HELEN

of

TROY

Tess Collins

BearCat
PRESS

Casebound: 978-1-937356-00-2
Trade paper: 978-1-937356-01-9
Kindle: 978-1-937356-02-6
EPUB: 978-1-937356-03-3
Library of Congress Control Number: 2011911039

Publisher's Cataloging-in-Publication Data
Collins, Tess.
    Helen of Troy / by Tess Collins.
        p. cm.
    ISBN: 978-1-937356-00-2
    1. Mythology, Greek—Fiction. 2. Helen of Troy (Greek mythology)—Fiction. 3. Appalachian Region—Fiction.
I. Title.
PS3603.O4558 .H45 2012
813—dc22
        2011911039

Published by BearCat Press: www.BearCatPress.com
BearCat Press logo by Golden Sage Creative
Book and cover design by Marin Bookworks

This book is dedicated to a big bunch of cousins, most of whom I know and some I'm still meeting but growing up in a big family was like living in Crazytown.
Best time I ever had.
Hope I didn't forget anybody.

The Collinses: Bruce Collins, Helen Latiff Coleman, Joddy Collins, Judy Hiscock, Okie Lee Turner Wolfe, and Sandy Robertson.

The Cosbys: Andrea Cline Gibbs, Brad Cosby, Cindy Cosby, David Frohwerk, Joann Knight, Jody Cosby, Joey Cosby, Kaye Cosby, Lana Cosby, Mary Ann Cosby, Melissa Hardin, Regina Cosby Schneider, Robin Cline, Shane Love, Veronica Cosby, and Wayne Cosby.

And in memory of the ones we lost: Cheryl Cosby, Michael Collins, Mike Cosby, Norman Knight and Sharon Cosby.

Also special thanks to the very wise James N. Frey, Waimea Williams, and Tashery Shannon; And to Earl Gilbert who worked in Uncle Sam's grocery store and reminded me that it was cornmeal I used to write my name in on that butcher block.

HELEN

of

TROY

1

Nobody in the county, let alone the state of Tennessee, would have laid down even money on me and Rudy Ramsey ending up married. My great-grandmother Dottie and his great-uncle Ernie caused considerable scandal when they eloped before she'd divorced her husband. With the law hot on their heels because Ernie was a month shy of sixteen, they got as far as Chattanooga before being hauled back and thrown in Claiborne County jail. He was released to his parents, while twenty-year-old Dottie fought charges of immoral behavior and corrupting a minor.

Twenty-nine days and eight hours later, Ernie celebrated his birthday by stealing his Uncle Joe's motorbike. He and Dottie disappeared forever, leaving behind her fed-up husband and four squalling kids. Far as anybody ever knew, Dottie never got that divorce. After all this time it's easy to think of their affair as romantic, but my forbearers' taint followed me when Rudy's Aunt Birdy whispered at my bridal shower that wildness just might run in the veins of the Aubrey women and Rudy better think twice before marrying me. I didn't take kindly to that and I called her out, waiting for two hours in the town square, ready to whip her good. She might have been a fifty-year-old woman, but if she was old enough to insult me, she was young enough to fight me.

The only time I ever got whipped was when I was seven. I'd gotten into my mother's make-up, powdering my face, streaking my cheeks pink with rouge. Blue eye shadow ringed my eyes and my lips were a wet, scarlet bow. Momma took a hickory switch to my legs. The humiliating blows stung like bees. "I'll beat that hot, wild blood out of you!" she cried, then dragged me to the sink and rubbed a washcloth around my face until the skin was raw. "You're vain, Helen Aubrey. Pride is the devil's mirror." Those final words never stuck with me. It was my hot, wild blood that fixed in my mind. As I grew older I often traced the veins on the back of my hands and wondered where those fiery and untamed rivers would lead me.

My husband Rudy and I have run Troy Hardware in Eastern Tennessee since his mother died last summer and left him the business. It's a slender building with a high ceiling and a gray, unfinished floor worn down in the aisles from customers who have traded here for the last eighty years. These blanched green walls have stories to tell of how Elvis Presley bought a fan belt when his car overheated right in the middle of the town's intersection. That was before he was famous so nobody paid him any mind, and Rudy's daddy helped him fix the car. John F. Kennedy also stopped to use the bathroom when he was on his Appalachian tour. He rolled through town in a black limousine that some said was half a block long. For years the hand towel that Senator Kennedy used hung framed in a place of honor beside family pictures of four generations of Ramseys. It disappeared one night after Rudy's high-school graduation party. Much as we all hated to admit it, most of us believed Rudy's best friend Raleigh Lynch had thrown up and carelessly used the towel to clean up the mess.

A tin Pepsi thermometer nailed beside the door is autographed by Jane Russell, and several bullet holes line the arch over the tractor parts, left from a shoot-out between revenuers and moonshiners—the store just happened to get caught in the middle. There's even a faded bloodstain on the brown Masonite counter where Rudy's great-grandfather was wounded during a robbery. Townsfolk always claimed that Al Capone held up Troy Hardware while passing through to Knoxville, but after I married Rudy I found out it was Nelson Pitt, a no-account cousin that his family disowned.

Troy, Tennessee is perched at the peak of Waldemar Mountain, west of Pruden and east of Jellico in Clearfork Valley. Not much in this area but snaky roads leading around abandoned coal mines, sharp ridges and steep cliffs that shelter the ancient hollows of the Appalachian highlands. Named after a great city with mythic warriors and beautiful princesses, Troy has nothing like that. We've never been sacked, looted or overrun by invading armies.

In our Troy, hardly anything ever changes. The population has been between two hundred sixty-eight and two seventy-five for at least a decade. Our people work in the mines, on farms, at the rock quarry, in the ministry and government service. Almost every household has a garden patch and if the frost gets your tomatoes, somebody will give you their extras. Everyone knows everyone else's names. We watch the news on television, listen to country music on Knoxville stations, and a few of us talk by CB radio to the truckers on I-75. We gossip and philosophize, pray and complain, yet all the troubles of the world rarely affect Troy. Inflation might rise, the economy might flounder, wars are fought and peace is made, but life here is as constant as a river that's never seen a heavy rain.

From my kitchen window I can see Hazel's Beauty Shop, where I have my hair set once a week, and an army-navy store where Mr. Henderson leaves his checkerboard set up in the front window and if he's in the middle of a game when you need something, then count on waiting until he's won. Yvonne Couasonon's diner is across the street and she regularly hangs out a handwritten sign claiming her Grandma Sissy invented cornbread in that kitchen. The streets fill out with a drug store, three dress shops, a dentist, and a locked-up lawyer's office that to my knowledge has never opened for business. If anyone from Troy was ever in a courtroom, they've kept it a secret.

At the outskirts of our town is a gallery for a dozen artisans who ferry their folk art and crafts to places like Gatlinburg and Cumberland Gap, and sell them at county fairs and museums. Most of the buildings in the center of town were built in the early 1900s from stands of thousand-year-old forests of white oak, basswood, birch, ash, hickory, maples and tulip poplars. The post office and a school are the only redbrick buildings, anchoring the east and west blocks, and an unkempt park and Baptist church box in the north and south sides. Reverend Johnnie Studen has baptized most of us in Clear Fork Creek, and he reads Psalm 121 over us after we've been laid to rest.

Having a corner lot at the town's sole intersection is a good location and we're the only hardware store between Jellico and Fork Ridge, so it's easier for people on all sides of us to drive here than risk the winding roads of the Cumberland Mountains to the larger towns. We have a thriving little business with locals, from farmers to auto repairmen to the average citizen in need of a plunger. We serve not only the small number of people in our unincorporated community but most everybody within sight of the mountain.

We have pretty good friends and neighbors despite that for a generation our ancestral lovebirds were a real sore spot. The Ramsey and Aubrey clans wouldn't walk down the same side of the street or go shopping on the same day. But all that stopped before Rudy and I were born. My family became a row of tombstones and quaint names in a worn out Bible: Mattie Parmeda, Beulah Lambdin, Arly Dale, Marcus Dewey, Siler Lee. More than fifty others were now no more than faded ink on yellow, brittle paper. Except for the stories of old-timers, I could only imagine what kind of lives my ancestors led. Most of the Ramseys went north to the big cities of Cleveland and Detroit, chasing assembly-line jobs they hoped would lead to union pensions. Rudy's line, however, stayed in the Cumberland Mountains. I guess that was lucky for me—but I swear there were days when it sure didn't feel like it.

Two weeks after my thirty-eighth birthday, and I'd spent the time since then scrubbing shelves and dusting the overstocked summer patio furniture. Rudy was supposed to clean the store's awning, but I could hear him upstairs in our apartment, grunting at the televised football game every few minutes.

"Rudy!" I yelled up the stairs. "We're never gonna be ready for the Thanksgiving Sidewalk Sale if you don't get down here and help."

"I'm fixing the cable." He followed that with, "It's too cold to crawl out on the roof. I'll do it next summer."

I threw down my dust rag and rolled my eyes. Bootlegging the cable was what he meant. Once upon a time, he'd have come running like a hound for supper at the sound of my voice. He'd start every day by rising first, then wake me up with a mug of coffee steaming under my nose. At bedtime he'd brush my hair and massage my shoulders. Some nights he'd play his guitar until I fell asleep, and before I married him, he even wrote a song called "Helen of my Heart." That's when I figured I'd better love this man.

Those were the days before sports infected his blood.

Now it's not much use trying to get any work out of him when the University of Tennessee Volunteers play football, or during a Kentucky Wildcats basketball game, or if any southern team's having a good year. That left a few odd weeks between sports seasons when I might get his attention. "Ru-dee," I called out again, but it had no fire to it because I knew it was hopeless. In the back where a storage room shared space with what we called the kitchen, I put the kettle on the burner. A few minutes later I settled into an old Appalachian sittin' rocker with a cup of warm water.

The leaves outside the window were starting to turn brown and soon winter would take them all. But right now, some were still changing colors. Red, gold, orange and purple, some a fade of wash, creating hues that even my artist friend, Rachel, could never duplicate, and she's as good as you can find in these parts. I wished I could change as easy as those leaves. But then, they didn't really do anything but live their lives, did they? Their transformation happened just like popping corn. Every year I watched their magic and couldn't help but be envious.

Across the street, a man who looked vaguely familiar pulled a rental truck up to the side of Troy Market. He got out and started unloading boxes at the rear entrance. It led up to the apartment above. I leaned the rocker back a littler farther to see what was going on. A rusted, half-fallen Stucky's Diner sign pointing toward the freeway blocked my view.

Workmen had been constructing something on top of

the store for a week now. The owner had retired to Florida and rumors going up and down Troy's two intersecting streets said his son, Garland, was moving back home from Knoxville to take over. Cassandra Dimsdale, the local postmistress, was Garland's sister and she told Joan Jackson who told Rachel Kincaid who told Maude Fletcher who told me that her brother was looking for a quieter kind of life. Well, he'd sure find it in Troy. He was six years older than me as I was growing up, so I didn't remember much about him.

One memory remained strong. I was twelve when everybody living on the mountain fought a fire that almost destroyed the town. I helped fill buckets from a fountain in front of the church. When I turned to hand off my bucket, the sight of leaping flames sent a rod of fear through me and I stood there paralyzed. This gangly eighteen-year-old boy, singed eyebrows and soot-ringed nostrils, took my bucket and jiggled my arm, breaking me from my trance. Our eyes fixed on each other's. His irises were the dark blue of the sky melting into dusk. I reached out and touched his cheek. He nodded but didn't speak. I held my breath as he rushed back to the burning building. In that moment, knowing he might die, I yelled out, "Be careful!" He left town not long after that. I don't believe we ever spoke again, but even at twelve years old, I knew I'd been in the company of a hero.

Now movers were unloading furniture off the truck outside of Troy Market. A premonition of something terrible bubbled in my veins. I shook it off, blaming it on staying too long in the memory of the fire. No reason to be nervous about Garland Cookson moving back to town. It was as much his town as mine. Still, my insides filled with a need for caution as if I were getting ready to walk a narrow plank.

I've lived here since I was eight with Maude Fletcher, who took in orphans for the state. She was like my mother and was surely my best friend. When most of my graduating class decided to leave this mountaintop perch, she offered to pay my way through beauty school. I was all set to attend Collins School of Cosmetology in Middlesboro, Kentucky and thought maybe some day I might even open my own shop. Rudy was headed to college at Lincoln Memorial University, only three miles from there, but his father fell ill and he stayed to help his mother. The next night he asked me to marry him. Looking into his eyes, somehow I saw how lonely he'd be without me and I couldn't bear for him to feel that emptiness. So, I stayed in Troy. Though I never told anyone, my daydreams were always about what might have happened to me if I'd tried my luck at the world.

"Helen!" Rudy yelled without even coming to the staircase. "Make me a burnt baloney sandwich."

Damn! He had this way of always asking for something right when I'd found the most comfortable position. But it was a reasonable enough request considering I hadn't made lunch. I pushed myself up out of the rocker, fetched the bread and baloney from the refrigerator, turned on the burner and leaned back, expecting flames to pop up. All I got was a hiss of gas.

"Pilot light's out," I called up. "Come down here and fix it."

His heavy footsteps on the stairs were accompanied by a frustrated, "I swear to God. . . ." He bounced into the kitchen like a locker room jock in his orange UT sweatshirt and boxer shorts.

"Put some pants on. What if a customer comes in."

"They'd just tell you what a lucky woman you are." He grinned like a fool, ran his fingers through blond hair thinning at the crown, and winked, then bent, pulled open the oven and sniffed. "Can't figure why you don't learn to do this yourself."

"You know fire spooks me."

"It's silly that a grown woman won't hold a match to her own pilot light." He checked the broiler, then pulled up the top counter. "It's only the top part." He struck a match against the side of the stove and held it to the burner.

The puff of blue flame shot up and he smirked at me like it was the easiest thing in the world. Taking a Budweiser from the refrigerator, he headed back to the football game. I placed the frying pan on the burner and dropped in a slice of butter. The flame whizzed like someone had sucked it in.

"It went out again," I called to him.

He came around the corner and kicked the stove. Then kicked it again.

"That's not gonna make it light," I said.

"I hate it when the dern thing does that. I lit it three times yesterday. Dern thing should stay lit when I light it."

I stood back while he worked on the pilot once more, wondering if he'd added another dent. A half-dozen dings on the side and four more on the front had started to rust. Rudy was only responsible for about three of them. His father had left the others. Ramsey men had this way of taking their frustrations out on the furniture. In the time I've lived in this building, we'd thrown out four lopsided bookshelves, six sinks and twelve television sets. After Rudy's dad took a baseball bat to a leaking toilet he'd been unable to fix, we found ourselves without a bathroom the whole month of December. My mother-in-law finally issued an ultimatum to her wheelchair-bound husband, "You're not a carpenter, a plumber or a TV repairman, and if I catch you trying to act like one again, it'll be me losing my temper and it won't be household furnishings I'm kicking!" She had smiled a sad smile in my direction as if she knew I'd have to learn to deal with the famous Ramsey temper in my own way.

These days Rudy always seemed to be mad at something, even if it was only the stove. When that happened, all I could do was wait. His brown and black beagle, Myrtle, came in from the room off the kitchen and that seemed to calm him down. After Rudy got the burner going again, he said, "Hello boy, hello boy, what's ya doin'?" then he picked up the piece of baloney I was about to fry. "Here, have this."

"Don't give him that," I objected, too late, "he'll never eat dog food again." The slice disappeared in one bite.

"This dog's my best buddy," he said. "I tell him all my secrets, even my Swiss bank account number. We go hunting, fishing and canoeing. If it's good enough for me, it's good enough for Myrtle."

"Well, then, your dog is the only one getting a baloney sandwich 'cause you just fed him the last piece."

Rudy looked at me then back at the empty package sitting on the table. "Blast it, Helen, why didn't you say something?"

"Well, I figured if Myrtle could take it as a bribe, he might give me them Swiss bank numbers and I'll go out and buy an electric stove."

He studied me for a few seconds, somehow knowing he'd been insulted but not quite wanting to accuse the woman who cooked for him. "Well, run across the street and get some more baloney."

"You run across the street and get more baloney. I been working and scrubbing all day while your lazy hind end's been watching television."

"Don't smart-mouth me, woman."

"Or you'll do what?" He shut up good and quick. But now I was peeved. I marched forward, always able to back down a big mouth, and he stumbled two steps backwards. "Come on, Mr. Tough-Guy, you'll what?"

"All I wanted was a baloney sandwich."

"No, all you wanted was a burnt baloney sandwich."

"What's wrong with you?"

"With me?" For a second I saw myself running him through with the butter knife in my hand. I squeezed it and must have had a dangerous look on my face cause the dog got up and moved to the door, tail between his legs. "I'll tell you. Six o'clock this morning the alarm went off. Seven to ten I stickered sales prices on the summer inventory. Ten to twelve I swept the sidewalk, watered the flower box and tried to spray the bird dung off the awning. Twelve to two I pulled those kiddie swimming pools that I told you not to order from the storeroom, and stacked them up real pretty out front. Two to four I restocked the bags and packing, did a bank deposit, and in between all this waited on fifteen customers. I haven't eaten, sat down or pissed all day, and I reckon you could say I've just about had it."

Rudy crossed his arms over his chest and cocked his head to one side. His pale blue eyes narrowed and his lower lip stuck out. "You know what you need, Helen. You need a baby."

That stopped me cold. I stood there staring, trying to comprehend what he'd really said and half thinking I'd heard wrong.

"A baby would keep you occupied. It'd delight and enter-tain you. You wouldn't be so upset all the time." He walked around me, looking up and down my body. "Besides that, it's about time I got me a namesake."

Those last words caught my attention, all right. "You want something named after you, honey, take that hound dog sitting right there over to the county courthouse, and change its name to Rudy Ramsey, Jr. 'cause that's as close to a namesake as you're gonna get in this house!"

I stormed out to the front, put the closed sign on the door, then shut myself in the bedroom and didn't come out the rest of the evening. When I woke up several hours later, Rudy was snoring away next to me. He had baloney breath so

I figured he'd gotten his sandwich. I turned my back to him, eyes wide open, unable to sleep.

Baby, I thought, that's a subject that hadn't reared its bald head in a while. We'd always planned on having a child. Sometimes I wondered how so much time passed without us noticing that another year was gone and no patter of little feet. Early in our marriage I could blame work. "Next month," one of us would say. "We'll start a family next month." Another season would roll by and I began to grow irritated with Rudy's forgetfulness, his messiness, his stubborn temper. Part of me wasn't sure I wanted a baby who might inherit those Ramsey traits. It's not that I meant to avoid him but I know I did.

Then one day, Selma Hanks came into the store. She must have been in her late thirties, thin and bird-like with salt-and-pepper hair. She had a tired, droopy-eyed look as if she'd given up on the world. Rudy waited on her, but from the back of the store I could see from his expression that something was wrong.

I came forward and realized he was staring at ten of her fifteen children. Eight of them were lined up in height order right to the side of her. They squirmed and bit, punched and pinched. She'd holler at them, and they'd be good for about ten and a half seconds. She had another on her hip and an infant in a carriage. Then Rudy smiled. His wide, crap-eatin' grin that he shoots off when he's real uncomfortable. I found myself worried about him, wondering why I'd never even given him one child. His smile stayed frozen in place a good three minutes after she left. He never said anything and I never asked.

I shifted in bed and looked at his profile. Sometimes he was a man I didn't know. Babies, I thought again. Odd that he'd mention that today. Oh, well, he'll forget all about it by morning.

2

I held up a garland made from several old Christmas wreaths and a bunch of unused scarves. "What do you think of this to drape along the awning out front?" Maude, Rachel and her ten-year-old daughter Tansy eyed it.

"There's value in oddity," Rachel said, brushing back her coffee-colored bangs. Maude was silent and Tansy blinked twice then went back to reading her book.

"Fine." I dropped it into a garbage pail and continued pawing through another box of decorations.

"Look for something with a Thanksgiving theme." Maude leaned back in a lawn chair we had on sale, twirling the loose end of a bandanna around her head. Chemotherapy had taken her silver hair but at sixty-two she had one of the youngest faces I'd ever seen, with smooth, unwrinkled skin. Fleshier now from the drugs, she used them as an excuse to eat sweets and wear Muumuus. "If the world ends tomorrow," she always said, "my one regret would be that I never ate enough Oreos."

Right when I found a papier-mâché turkey, Rudy came sauntering in from his rumpus room—that extra space off the kitchen. It used to be his mother's bedroom, but he reclaimed it a month after the funeral and filled it with a pool table, free weights, a popcorn machine, and a beanbag couch. His buddies from the Eagan Coal Mine congregate there more times than I was happy with. It was also where Myrtle slept. "Ya'll running off the customers?" he asked jovially, biting into a fried chicken drumstick.

Rachel pursed her lips at him, narrowing her eyes with a studying look. "Honeybunch, they see us three Amazons in here and they'll throw down cash money." The two of them loved to spar. She was an artist, selling cartoon portraits and mountain landscape paintings to the museums in Gatlinburg.

"Rachel, sugar, keep your knees together, this ain't that kind of place." He tossed the chicken bone into a garbage pail and licked his fingers.

"Watch it," I warned, nodding toward Tansy.

"Rudy Ramsey, you've got the kind of smirk my Momma always threatened to smack off my face." Rachel sneered right back at him.

"Ya'll know we're gonna have a baby?" Rudy announced.

My mouth dropped open. "What?" I barely got it out before all the females jumped up and surrounded me.

"Why didn't you tell?"

"When's it due?"

"What're you going to name it?"

"Wait," I tried to say. "No, I mean. No."

My husband turned and headed toward his rumpus room.

"Come back here, Rudy Ramsey," I hollered. Everybody quieted down. "I am not pregnant." The Amazons sighed and returned to their starting places like disappointed children. I turned toward Rudy. "What do think you're doing?"

"We were talking about it, weren't we?"

"Were we?" I swallowed my irritation, not wanting to continue in front of my friends.

"Didn't mean to get you all excited," Rudy said sheepishly. "It started over a baloney sandwich." They all gave him perplexed looks but somehow knew better than to pursue the subject. "Garland Cookson burnt it right well for me." He pointed across the street toward the grocery store.

"Oh, Rudy, why'd you go bothering that man?" I asked. "He hasn't lived here since high school and the first thing he finds is you pestering him to cook a sandwich."

Rachel sat up straight. "You met him?"

"I don't like his face," Rudy said. "It's got no flaws." He jacked a knee up on a picnic table and leaned forward like an expert. "Looks like he's never had his nose broke or a tooth chipped. Got a lot of books over there and fancy flowers he moved around every time I started to light my cigar."

"You better not start smoking those stinky things again." I gave him a mean look.

"I'm kidding." He laughed. I doubt Rudy even liked

cigars, he just enjoyed threatening me with them.

Rachel and Maude shared one of those girl-looks like they were trying to compare Rudy's assessment with everything else they knew about Cookson and figure out if he was worth pursuing. Rachel wanted a husband, or at least a date.

But if they were going to girl-talk, better that Rudy not repeat all he heard to his gossipy buddies, and he would. "Husband, make yourself useful," I told him, "and clip this turkey to the top of the awning. Right in the middle. I left two clothespins up there last year. And get the ladder," I added as he opened the door. "Don't stand on my flower box."

He dinged the bell on his way out and jumped up on the flower box in one hop, balancing himself like an aerialist, then made a smirky face at me through the window.

"Why don't you have a baby?" Tansy asked. "I could be the sitter."

"Oh, honey," I said. "I'm too old for that."

"You are not." Maude gave me an admonishing look. "I think you're either vain or just afraid to get pregnant." Rachel nodded in agreement but I could tell her mind was on the new man across the street.

Just then Rudy lost his balance, landing in a thud accompanied by a rousing round of cuss words. "Besides," I said as he got up and jumped right back on the flower box. "I've already got that kid." He held on to the navy-colored awning and dropped the turkey twice before getting it to hold. "You know, if his Momma could see what he's done to her bedroom she'd get up out of her grave and pitch a fit."

"Rudy's rumpus room is the funnest place in town," Tansy said, bringing the conversation back to a cheery tone. "He taught me how to shoot pool that day you all went to Juanita's Beauty Shop over in Middlesboro."

"You're going to be a teenager in a few years," I told her, "and you've got to be smarter about what you say in front of your mother." I rubbed her head and tugged one of her brown pigtails.

"I do it cause I'm a smart-aleck." Tansy put her hand over her face to hide a grin.

Rachel rolled her eyes and shook her head. "Her sassy mouth almost got her kicked out of Sunday school last week."

"It wasn't my fault, Momma." Tansy looked at Maude and me for support.

"I'm sure it wasn't," we both said, nodding our heads. There wasn't much we wouldn't do for Tansy.

"What'd you do to old Sandy Dimsdale?" Maude asked, leaning forward.

"We have to call her Miss Cassandra." Tansy grimaced at the memory.

"Honey, you get the kids all calling her Miss Sandy as fast as you can. She hates that."

"Maude," I warned, "you're gonna get this child in trouble." I could hardly contain my amusement but tried hard for the sake of the girl. "Now, tell us what happened." We all leaned forward like a big secret was about to be told.

"Well—" Tansy shivered and folded her hands in front of her.

"Take deep breaths," I said, stroking her back.

"I'd rather take a Valium," Rachel piped up

"Not you, silly." I rubbed Tansy's shoulder and sat down beside her.

"Cassandra Dimsdale gives me the creeps." Rachel shuddered, then pretended to spit in disgust. "She's mean as sour apples."

Maude twirled one hand, motioning Tansy to get on with the story.

"Miss Cassandra was telling us about Jesus and the Romans," Tansy explained, "then she asked if we knew how Rome got its name. I raised my hand but she ignored me."

Maude and I shared a look. We both knew ole Sandy was prejudiced against poor kids, especially Tansy. Part of it was because of rumors that Rachel had had an affair with Cassandra's husband five years ago. I didn't know if it was true, and if Maude did, she never let on. But I could see how a man would stray after living with *Sandy the harpy*, as many in town called her behind her back. Rachel was a fun-loving, thirty-year-old flirt but a good mother to little Tansy. Push comes to shove, I doubted she ever followed up on her playful come-ons. In a small town, flirting can appear like a full-blown affair without anything ever happening. Cassandra, on the other hand, was the kind of self-righteous biddy who'd take out her frustration on a ten-year-old girl.

"She told us about Romulus and Remus being suckled

by a she-wolf," Tansy continued. "And after that, the city was named Rome after Romulus. Then she went back to Jesus, but I raised my hand again and asked why it wasn't named Reme instead of Rome?'

"Always good to challenge authority now and then," Maude said, bobbing her head.

"The two brothers got into a fight and Romulus killed Remus." We all smiled and nodded. "She said her superior knowledge of mythology gave her the edge in teaching the Bible because she understood the interpretations of divine carnality."

"Well, how grand of her," Maude scoffed.

"Then I said that wasn't the half of it." Tansy leaned forward, her excitement growing. "She hadn't even gotten to the rape of the Sabine women!"

All three of us adults whooped out in laughter, unable to control ourselves. The thought of Cassandra Dimsdale being made a fool by a ten-year-old was enough to give us joy for a week.

"She got real upset, but look, it's all here." Tansy held up her Classical Mythology book and showed us a picture of toga-clad women fleeing from imperial-looking soldiers.

"That girl and her library books." Rachel shook her head, but also smiled, proud that she had somehow lucked out in giving birth to such a smart daughter.

"Here's you," she said to me, turning a few pages. "Helen of Troy." She pointed at a drawing of a woman with long, flowing blond hair, wearing a Roman dress adorned with gold shells, and gazing out in the distance like she saw a coming storm.

"It does kinda favor you, Helen," Maude said, looking over Tansy's shoulder.

"Well, saints above." Rachel held the book up next to my face and studied my features. "It's a spitting image. Here you are, Helen of Troy."

"Helen of Troy, my foot," said a voice mixed with the dinging of the doorbell. "I was voted Mayfair Princess two years in a row."

"Come on in, Cassandra," I replied flatly. "Join the fun."

The bow at the collar of her coat looked tight enough to choke and gave her a double chin, but her jaw-length, amber-blond hair distracted from the slack in her jowls. She *had* been a beauty in her day and her slightly upturned nose gave a hint of the perky girl she used to be. She tapped a clipboard with a pen and walked toward us. With a nod to Maude, and a slight acknowledgment of Tansy, but ignoring Rachel completely, she proclaimed, "I didn't come for fun."

"Naturally," Maude said.

"I came to make sure you replace Mary Margaret's awful carrot cakes with some kind of decent dessert for the After-Sale-Day party."

"There's a pudding sample right back in the kitchen," I volunteered, "you can test it."

"This is going to be one of the best organized town shindigs ever," Rachel remarked.

Cassandra turned her back on Rachel and bent over to

straighten a pant cuff. Now even in a small town, turning your butt upward toward somebody is bad manners, if not an outright insult, and I felt it was high time Sandy got over something that probably hadn't even happened. "It's called pomegranate surprise," I blurted to get everybody's attention off Cassandra's backside, then ran back to get the dessert. "Let's try it." I smiled wide and handed out five spoons.

We all took a dip and some "Mmmms" followed.

Rachel kept quiet, then stepped directly into Cassandra's line of sight. "I'm sorry, Helen, but I've got to tell the truth. It tastes just like a johnson after it's been in a sock."

Cassandra's eyes flared and if lightning could have struck, its flash would not have matched the glares between the two women. I knew Rachel didn't mean what she'd said about the pudding, but was just trying to shock old Sandy. I reached for a dime from the cash register and handed it to Tansy. "Honey, run across the street and get yourself a fudgesicle."

"Are they going to fight like Kilkenny cats?" she asked.

"What, pray tell, is a Kilkenny cat?" Cassandra towered over the little girl.

The three of us surrounded Cassandra like tough cookies about to intimidate an opponent, but Tansy stood her ground and quoted the old English verse:

"'There once were two cats at Kilkenny.

Each thought there was one cat too many.

So, they quarreled and fit.

They scratched and they bit,

so excepting their nails and

the tips of their tails,

Instead of two cats there weren't any.'"

"Humph." Cassandra tapped her pen on the clipboard and squinted.

"Was that a good joke or have I had too many martinis?" Rachel anchored one arm on her hip and let one foot tap in time with Sandy's pen. "You know the Martini brothers, don't you?"

I quickly ushered Tansy out the door and told Rudy to stay away too. One look at who was inside, and he followed Tansy. By the time I turned back around, Rachel and Cassandra were face to face, and Maude was holding each of them by an arm.

"I don't recall speaking to you," Cassandra informed Rachel. "I didn't even come in here to see you, and you've got no right to—"

"But you're the main entertainment of my day."

"I am nothing to your day."

"You can say that again."

"Once again, you've proven that brains do not grow on trees." Cassandra looked at Maude and me. "If you had an ounce of self-respect, you'd find a better class of friend." She wagged a finger at us as if delivering a prophecy. "Mark my words. Trash begets trash, so don't be surprised if one day this friendship turns into trash."

"And you've shown there's nothing more hateful than a bitter person." Rachel put a hand dramatically over her heart like she'd learned something.

"You should be embarrassed to act this way in public. Taking advantage of the few friends you have in this town." Turning to me and Maude, she whispered loudly, "Don't say I never warned you."

Rachel tapped both cheeks with her index fingers. "Blush-proof."

"That's the way of it with women like you."

"Why don't you just roll up and die?"

"I pray for it daily." Cassandra looked up as if beseeching Heaven. "When my trials are over, the good Lord will bless the pure and the righteous."

"Gee," Rachel mocked, "I thought in this day and age virginity was a bad memory."

"The only bad memories I have are of you and your impertinent little daughter," Cassandra whipped back, "and better if the town was rid of the both of you."

"You bitch!"

"Well, doesn't that just explain everything!" Cassandra held open her arms, a swell of triumph spreading across her face. She pushed her bobbed blonde hair back from her forehead and twirled around as if modeling a gown. "Mark my words," she said again.

Rachel raised a fist, but I moved quickly to drag her toward the kitchen and out the back door. I assumed Maude did the same to Cassandra, in reverse and using the front. I stroked Rachel's shoulder. Her eyes brimmed with tears. "You have to ignore old Sandy," I said. "She only runs the town in her own mind."

"She makes me so mad sometimes I could knock the crap out of her," Rachel said, her hands shaking. "What makes her like that? She's in the clover. It's not like I got anything of hers."

I looked down at the ground. Rachel covered her face, and her cheeks colored red. "You don't owe me an explanation," I said.

"I never did anything with her husband." She turned aside, unable to look me in the eye. "I kissed him. That's all. I don't even know why. Drank too much beer at the Valentine's Day celebration."

"Rachel." I took her by the shoulders and gently shook her. "You're a beautiful woman, you got that sweet little girl. You could find a husband to take care of you both."

She wiped her nose and looked up at the sky. "In this town, ha!"

"I don't mean this to sound the wrong way." I paused, hoping to say the right thing. "Have you ever thought of leaving . . . going away, maybe just to a bigger town?"

She stared back for several seconds but didn't let loose on me. "Thought about it a lot. But if I left, it'd be 'cause Sandy Dimsdale ran me out and I just couldn't stand the idea of that."

I put my arm around her shoulders and led her down the walk. "She's a mean, jealous prude who'll find fault in everyone, and thinks she knows the way things ought to be."

Rachel blinked her watery eyes then put both arms

around my neck and hugged me. "I don't know what I'd do without you and Maude."

"I love you, too."

She sucked in a deep breath and let it out, smiling slightly, then looked over at the store where Tansy sat on the porch with Rudy. Both were eating fudgesicles. "I ought to go over there and introduce myself to Cassandra's brother."

"Don't ask for trouble you don't need." I chuckled at the thought but knew the right thing was to discourage her.

"Yeah, a man not married at his age has got to have something wrong with him." She waved to Tansy, who sprang up and ran toward her. "By the way, that pudding was yummy." They walked off, arms around each other, an endearing picture of mother and daughter.

Tansy turned to blow a kiss at me. "See you later, Helen of Troy."

I blew it back to her.

Back in the store I realized Tansy'd forgotten her library book. I hurried outside with it, but they were already at the end of the street, about to step onto the path to their trailer near the studio Rachel shared with several other artists. I went back inside and turned to the picture of Helen of Troy, the most beautiful woman in the world; the face that launched a thousand ships, and, according to Tansy's book, a daughter of the ancient god Zeus.

Curiously I looked in the mirror. My hair was my best feature, long and blond, soft as corn silk, and when the sun hit it just right, it glistened. If my face was pretty, it had a milky kind of comeliness, fair, pale, almost translucent. I'd always thought coffee brown eyes were uninteresting but Rachel once said it was a study in contrast. Soft lines spread around my eyes, but none on my lips, forehead or cheeks. Not like Cassandra Dimsdale and she was only three years older. Her hair was like straw from over-bleaching and her mouth was as lined as a prune. She'd been beautiful, County Mayfair Princess at seventeen and eighteen. No one had ever won two years in a row. But now she looked like a dried-out corn stalk. Sourness had sucked her dry from the inside.

I touched the soft wrinkles around my eyes. Maybe I looked older than I thought. Maybe I was just fooling myself. Who was I kidding? I was middle-aged; thirty-eight times two made seventy-six. "I get older faster and faster," I said to my reflection. Helen of Troy. I was Helen of Keep-on-Trying.

Rudy peeked in the front door, holding the bell so it wouldn't ding. "Them witches fight like Kilkenny cats?"

"They're gone," I told him. "You can come home."

He pushed back the lawn chair display where Rachel and Maude had been sitting and came up behind me, putting his arms around my waist. His lips nuzzled one of my ears and he tickled the lobe with his tongue. "Sure am glad we don't fight like that."

I chuckled. He could make me laugh at the oddest things. "But we do fight like that, worse sometimes." I put a hand on his thigh and pulled it a little tighter against mine. I started to bring up whether or not we'd had a discussion about babies but something inside of me held back. I decided to wait and see if he brought it up.

"Aw, we fuss but we don't mean it." He kissed my neck, biting softly on my shoulder. "Race you to the bedroom?"

"We got another hour before closing time." I could feel him against my backside, and moved a little, making him groan. "You liked that, huh."

"Let's close early."

"Go on upstairs," I said. "I'll lock up."

3

——

"It's not that I didn't want to. . . ." Rudy halfheartedly explained.

"Don't worry about it, honey."

"I tell you, one of these days they're going to make pills for that. Mark my words."

"Ugh." I shuddered, recalling the last time I heard the *mark my words*. "You sound like Cassandra Dimsdale about to deliver another one of her predictions."

"What'd Miss I-Know-Better-Than-You start up about now?"

"Oh, the usual, telling everybody what they *ought* to do, all according the law of Cassandra."

"Come here, baby," he said, drawing me up in his arms. He kissed my forehead and ran his fingers around my cheek. Soon his breath became slow and regular, and before long he was asleep. For a few minutes it seemed like we were back in high school, wrapped around each other, lying under a wild cherry tree that grew deep in the woods. We'd meet there every day in the summer, eat what fruit we could reach and then kiss until our heavy breathing told us we needed more. Beneath the thick-leafed branches we made love for the first time. We weren't married, but we never felt it as shame. "If I lived on the other side of the world, I'd still have found you," he told me, and a good ten years into our marriage we'd return there every summer and make love again.

I knew Rudy felt bad and I never said anything, but trying to make love without success was a regular occurrence in this bed. I'd thought once that maybe it was because the room had been his parents', so I painted it pale lavender and sprinkled cinnamon glitter on the ceiling so it glowed like stars. It was romantic and I did what I could to make it our room. It worked for the most part, but on the times it didn't, I couldn't help but worry about what would happen the next time we tried to make love.

Rudy's mother had been kind enough to give us this part of the house after her husband died, and she moved to the room beside the kitchen. I sorta felt guilty when he turned it into a rumpus room after her death, but I guess a man does need a place to go where his wife isn't in his face all the time. He'd been working out with a set of barbells and the muscles in his arms and chest were hard lumps. I ran my hand down his chest, resting it on his equally firm thigh. Kissing his shoulder and licking up the curve of his neck, I hoped he'd respond. His eyelashes flickered. False alarm. He was deep into dreaming—*dreaming about babies?*

I slipped out of his hold and sat up in bed. The house vibrated an unearthly quiet. The cluttered room oozed claustrophobia. Four upstairs rooms here, including a bathroom, and each of them packed like a nest. All too small for a family. Good thing we'd never had a baby, it'd be right there on top of us. I didn't know how Rudy'd managed with two older brothers. They left Troy as soon as they were old enough. Rudy stayed, helped in the store, and took over after his father died. Both of us cared for his mother during her long illness. We'd never been on a vacation or even a honeymoon, and the occasional trip to Knoxville was always combined with business. Sometimes it seemed like all life was, was work. I didn't know how a baby could have fit in to all that.

A light flashed past, startling me. It was colorful and I didn't quite see it full on, more out of the side of one eye. I pulled on a robe and went over to the window to look into the backyard. We had a pretty good size patch with a rusted swing set, a picnic table and our beat-up truck in the far corner. Rudy and his brothers had built a tree house in the beech tree but it had fallen apart through the years, and I wouldn't walk under it for fear of getting knocked in the head with a piece of wood.

A colorful prism of light flashed again. I put on shoes, went downstairs and carefully crept out into the yard. Whatever it was seemed to be coming from the moon. Then I realized that all the lights were rainbows, too beautiful to fear. They were the size of butterflies and each time I reached out to touch one it flew away as if eluding a child. The night was cold but I couldn't help dancing around under them, in them, through them. Soon there were more and more. I tried to follow their origin and again and again my gaze came to the full moon. Whatever was between the moon and me was creating moonbows. Dozens of kaleidoscopic colors intersecting, dangling, whipping around like fireflies. I twirled in a circle, my robe falling open, my hair tousled loose. Behind the yard's high fence I cavorted like Lady Godiva, absolutely certain nobody could see me.

Well, almost nobody. I stared up at the full moon, wondering where this unexpected gift could be coming from. Then, I saw Garland Cookson up on his roof. He used something to catch the light of the moon to make prisms. He was looking down, directly at me.

Our eyes met and I yanked my robe closed. Oh Lord, I felt like a fool. He continued staring at me. Then, he smiled. From what I could see of him from a distance, he was a tall, wide-chested man, brown headed and full through the jaw. His mouth was on the thin side, but that made his smile a little bigger and it was an appreciative one. Not leering, but a look that said he knew he'd just witnessed the dance of a goddess.

I scampered back inside, uncertain why I was thinking those things and sure I'd be dying of embarrassment by morning. I would have to do something. This was Cassandra Dimsdale's brother, after all. For all I knew, he could be worse than her.

Upstairs, I crawled in next to Rudy. His body was warm and I snuggled up to him. My muscles trembled like a quivering tambourine, and I wasn't exactly sure why. He shifted, putting an arm around my neck. I lay in the crook of his elbow watching the window. The rainbows shimmered in the air like fairy beings until the moon moved to the other side of the sky. The words *Be careful* repeated in my mind until I fell asleep.

4

When the produce truck pulled up in front of Troy's grocery, I knew it was time to face up to last night's foolishness. The delivery man stacked a bushel of pomegranates out front—my pomegranates, specially ordered for the party in the town square at the end of the Thanksgiving Sidewalk Sale. Could I pay for them and look Garland Cookson in the eye after he'd seen me prancing around my backyard naked as a nymph? He might have already told people about my cavorting. What if he'd told Cassandra? My stomach jumped like grasshoppers. I could just foresee every person in Troy knowing about my silliness.

Well, I thought, might as well get this over with. I trotted across the street, not bothering with a coat, and waited while Garland signed for the produce. He looked up in my direction, recognizing me immediately, and a brief spark in his eyes instantly snuffed itself out. I got a shiver in my toes that went straight up my back, but I had to admire the way he acted. Okay, I decided, sometimes in small towns people know things but act like they don't. Maybe that's how he'd be. I could live with that.

"Morning," I said, holding out a hand and swallowing my nerves. A warm palm covered mine and my skin tingled like electricity was shooting through me. I couldn't help but smile and my knees felt rubbery, making it hard not to sway. He was taller than I'd thought, almost six four, and his half-moon eyes made it hard to see the color. But I remembered the exact hue. They were dark blue like a silhouette of the mountains at dusk. "I'm Helen of Troy."

He gazed at me with a puzzled expression. "I'm Garland of Groceries."

I realized what I'd said and stuttered, "I, I, I mean, sorry. I meant to say I'm Helen Ramsey. I don't know if you remember me. I was four or five years behind you in school." Trembling ran all through me. How could I have said something so stupid? His eyes sparkled in an admiring way so I knew he wasn't making fun of me. A strange sensation stirred deep in my stomach like an expansion and a contraction fighting with each other. For several seconds we stared into each other's eyes. I realized I needed to say something but my parted lips had trouble with words.

"Me, I mean, my husband and I operate the hardware store. You need any nails or hammers, just come on over." I rambled nervously, not sure of what I was saying, and the flushing heat that went through my groin made me want to turn and run.

"I remember you." Garland nodded with an amused grin that seemed to keep him from laughing out loud. "The little sis with the big brown eyes."

"Reckon you do remember." My breath caught in my throat as streams of tickling vibrations ran up and down my mid-section. "I've grown into my eyes."

"In the most wonderful of ways."

We stared at each other again, the quiet not uncomfortable. "If this is the way men act in the city, every woman in town is going to be sending their husbands here for polite lessons. Rudy could sure use some."

"I got reacquainted with your husband yesterday."

"He says you make a mean burnt baloney sandwich."

He chuckled. "My daddy taught me to make them and I enjoy one myself now and then."

"The weather's about to turn icy in a week or two so I hope your father's tucked in nice and warm down in Florida."

"Got him all set up last week." Garland looked around the store, which had lines of shelves filled with rusty canned produce and smelled like the dust from old flour bags. "Promised I'd put some razzle-dazzle in the old store."

"I hope that's not why you came back to Troy," I said, sniffing out gossip along with my own curiosity. "Not much goes on around here, and too much excitement would give this old place a heart attack."

"Peace and quiet will be my reward." He glanced away, one large hand reaching out and touching a jar of peppermint candy. It seemed for a second that he saw a place or a person he'd run away from, a sadness that had caught him in a memory he wanted to escape.

For a brief instant, I thought I saw it too, or felt it in some way. It was a hurt that he couldn't release, so I changed the subject. "I couldn't help noticing you've put something on the roof, something that looks like a crystal house." I pointed upward. "I know it sounds silly but when the moonlight goes through it, it sends all kinds of moonbows into my back yard."

"I'm so sorry. I can re-build it on the other side."

"No, no, no. It's beautiful."

He paused, looking directly into my eyes, then his gaze widened to take in my whole face. "Yes, it is," he said softly as if unaware of his own voice. But he was, because he looked down as if he wished he hadn't said it and gave me an involuntary smile.

I couldn't help but smile too, and looked away.

"It's a glass house actually," he said. "It must act as a prism on full moon nights." He motioned toward the steps, holding out his hand. "Come on, I'll show you."

He led me upstairs. The apartment above the store was almost the same as ours but had an extra bedroom toward the front. I glanced inside and noticed from the position of the window that he could see into our backyard. A narrower staircase led to the roof. He turned and took my hand in his to go up the creaky steps. He had a big hand and mine nearly disappeared in it. When he opened the door an explosion of sunlight made me cover my eyes, and I had to depend on him to lead me outside.

"My lord," I exclaimed as I took in what he'd built, a greenhouse filled with plants and flowers. We stepped inside. The warmth was like a humid summer day and filled my lungs with moist air.

"I swear by Jove that this time next year, the residents of Troy, Tennessee will have vine-ripened tomatoes in December."

That ambition was the least of it. His flowers were the most interesting I'd ever seen. I pointed at a dozen bat-shaped purple blossoms hanging from a shaded portion of the greenhouse. "What in the world?"

"Dracula Vampira," he said. "Orchids are my passion. Those are some of the more exotic. They grow in the dark part of the forest." He indicated more strange plants in pale lavender, creamy white, lime green, maroon. "Orchids are the largest group of flowering plants on earth. Twenty-five to thirty thousand species. Some are as small as only two inches high, but certain rainforest specimens are taller than me."

"Well, let's hope they don't plan on conquering the world."

"My goal is to get a first-class certificate from the American Orchid Society for my Tiger Orchid. It could take me years and a lot of careful work. Not to mention expense."

"All that trouble for a flower?"

"We call it orchid fever." He chuckled at himself. "These

flowers have been called the food of the satyrs, for obvious reasons."

I was staring at a bright red flower with pointed petals and a drooping sack that hung from the bottom of the bloom when it hit me what he meant. I hoped I wasn't turning bright red myself. "They're well-developed little fellas," was all I could manage to say.

"Here it is." He opened both hands wide, like presenting a rare jewel, and cradled an orange flower with large, flat petals delicately striped with black. "The lines haven't joined yet so they look more spotted, but I hope in five years or so that I'll have a winning hybrid."

"You created this?"

"A lot of patience created it." He touched one orange petal with the tenderness of someone caressing a child's cheek. "And over here," he pointed, "a dalliance, but I believe that's the source of the moonbow lights keeping you awake."

I lost my breath like fairies had stolen it. Beyond the orchids I walked among hundreds of crystals shaped like clovers, diamonds and snowflakes. They hung from the ceiling and caught the light in such unusual, interesting ways. I didn't know which way to turn because every direction was more beautiful than the last.

"I don't have time this week," he said, "but I'll re-hang them so they won't bother you."

"Don't you dare," I said, letting my hands caress the bottom edge of the crystals. "Last night was like waking up in the Garden of Eden."

"Well," he said, drawing out the word, "let's hope the apples taste as good as they look."

I hardly noticed what he'd said, but the quiet afterwards caused me to turn toward him. He was looking at me with a familiarity that made me feel flattered and a little bit special. And I didn't know why but it also made me hope that he'd invite me back again. "And that the serpents are friendly," I joked.

On the way back downstairs I noticed how clean and neat he kept the apartment. No dust on the mahogany dressers, beds made and covered with green chenille bedspreads, not a dirty dish in the sink. A set of pink flowered china with gold edges lined a shelf behind the dinner table. The plates were encased in glass and looked like they'd never been used. I liked seeing all this order 'cause it was a sign of a decent man. It also made me think he might be a little lonely. He needed a good woman, and I decided to take it upon myself to introduce him to someone. Rachel was a little too wild, no matter how much I might have wanted to help her out. Maybe that librarian who drove the bookmobile up here once a month from Jellico would be a good fit for him. Tansy was real fond of her. "I'll send Rudy over to get the pomegranates," I said, glancing at the bushel basket.

"No need," he said. "I'll carry it over."

"How nice of you." I studied his reflection in a mirror behind the counter. He'd grown into a handsome man, not exactly pretty the way I might think of Rudy, but interesting looking and deep. Suddenly there was another reflection behind him, not in the store, but outside. Peering in the corner of the window, eyes wide as quarters, mouth pinched like a dried-out mushroom, a spying spider in a web: Cassandra. "You're nothing like. . . ." I paused, catching myself about to say something rude.

"Like my sister," he finished my sentence.

"I'm sorry. I shouldn't have—"

"You didn't, I did." He crossed his arms, looking off to the side. "It's easy to stay in a place like Troy and act like a queen bee, but go out into the world, and control mavens like my sister manage to hurt themselves as much as they do others."

I wondered if the part of him that seemed sad wished for a different kind of life, not the one he'd led, or wanted to come back to in Troy, but to something totally different. I was too afraid to ask.

"The hard part is once you dispatch one of 'em, here comes another to take her place." He shook his head. "I've had some experiences."

"I reckon we've all got used to Cassandra. Seems most the time she's part of the background now. She whines, complains and tells us how we ought to be living, and we just go uh-huh."

He chuckled and nodded in agreement. "She and I only recently started speaking civil again after a five-year argument about my father's wish to retire to Florida."

"Looks like you got your way."

"My father got his wish. That's what counts. My sister

and I agreed that for his sake we'd try and get along. I'd like to keep this store running as a legacy to him for at least as long as he's alive."

I turned to go, as it seemed Cassandra was not coming inside. "Well, I'll see you soon, and make sure you try some of my pomegranate pudding at the party." I leaned down to pick up the basket and his hands covered mine.

"I'll carry it for you."

"No need." Suddenly I felt like I had no breath in me. Sensation consumed me like a fire eating up a dried tree. The warmth of his skin on mine, minty flavor of his breath and again, lost in the valley of his eyes. "I'll send Rudy over," I managed to say, and broke away from a connection I couldn't explain.

Outside, the cold air woke me up like coming out of a dream. I could see Cassandra trying to hide her scrawny carcass behind a post. If she'd spotted us coming down from the upstairs apartment it would be just like her to make something out of nothing. I started across the road and pretended I hadn't seen her.

"Miss Helen of Troy," Cassandra called out, having followed me out into the street.

"Would you not call me that, Sandy," I said, putting emphasis on the name she hated.

Her mouth was a thin line and her eyes were unblinking. "A little cold out here to be without a coat?"

"I only came across the street to check on my pomegranates."

"Well," she said with a drawl. "They're in the store, not in the upstairs apartment."

I smiled. Why explain how innocent it all was and give her any satisfaction? "Your handsome brother is going to bring them over to me." I continued on but heard her coming up behind me.

"And here all this time I thought it was that trampy little Rachel I'd have to worry about."

I whirled around. Half my body leaned toward her and the other half struggled to stay rooted to the ground

Her eyebrows peaked in that witchy way of hers. "Mark my words, dirt rubs off on those it associates with."

"I resent that, Cassandra Dimsdale."

"You ought to learn a lesson and go home to your own husband."

"You ever speak to me that way again, it won't be Rachel's footprint on your backside."

Our eyes locked but I won. Her stare was wary, as if she knew I would not hesitate to carry out such a threat. She humphed and turned, wagging her butt like a duck as she strutted off down the street.

5

——

I stomped across the street just fuming. If it'd been a dirt road I would have been kicking up dust. I was ready to fight the first person in my path.

Rudy stood outside staring up at the awning. "I think that turkey's lopsided," he remarked.

"That awning's been lopsided the last five years and you're just now noticing it?" My voice had an edge. He turned and looked at me peculiar. "I told you twelve dozen times to re-sew the canvas on the left side and did you? No, you leave it 'til 'next summer.'" I mocked him up and down.

"What's wrong with you?"

"Nothing," I said with a clip. "And don't you jump up on this flower box again." I banged my hand on the porch pole beside it. "I have to paint it every dern spring to get your dirty shoe prints off my white paint."

"Hold on now."

"It won't even wash off any more."

"Not all them footprints are mine."

"Yeah," I said, determined to let him have it. "Your buddies jump on it to cross over to the sidewalk. They see you doing it and then it's copycat city."

"Along with half the teenage boys in town." He shifted, grumbling like a child in trouble. "Like Cody Williams standing right yonder." He pointed at a lanky teenage boy with buckteeth who'd stopped to watch us fuss at each other. "Go on, Cody," Rudy said. "Show her how you jump up on the flower box to get to the sidewalk."

"You do that Cody Williams, and you'll spend the rest of your teenage years singing soprano."

The boy stood still as ice, his basset hound eyes going from one of us to the other. His hand unconsciously twisted the bottom of his *Let's Boogie* T-shirt into a knot. Several other people had gathered, a handful behind Rudy and a half dozen behind me.

"This has to do with last night, don't it?" His head cocked to the side.

"This has to do with my flower box, not whether you can get it up."

A sporadic laughter rose from both crowds. I could hardly believe what had passed through my lips. Rudy glanced tentatively over his shoulder and back at me. "I can salute just fine, Missy," he said. "You've just lost your touch on keeping it there."

Steam felt like it was puffing from my ears and everything I said next was like words in a foreign tongue. I came to myself saying, "The screwing I'm getting ain't worth the screwing I'm getting!"

Rudy reared back, took a run at the flower box and kicked it so hard it busted in pieces. Dirt spilled on the porch. The chrysanthemums tipped sideways. "Now I don't have to jump over on your damn flower box," he told me triumphantly.

Someone pushed through the crowd. I about died of embarrassment to see Garland, carrying the bushel of pomegranates. He eyed the smashed boards, set the basket to one side, and hurried over to me. "You okay, Helen?"

"Her?" Rudy exclaimed with a shocked stare. "I'm the one that 'bout broke my foot."

"Well, excuse me, Mr. Ramsey, but you did kick a flower box."

Rudy stood there open mouthed, not used to being told to accept responsibility.

The people gathered around us laughed and joked. "Why don't you come over to my house, Rudy," Dwight Sharp hollered, showing a side of gold teeth. "I'll let you kick my old outhouse. It needs to be tore down."

"Well, he can't leave," Randy Woods jeered, "his wife might not be here when he gets back!" The crowd roared with laughter.

I covered my face with both hands. Garland recognized my embarrassment, wrapped an arm around me, and led me inside the store. "These people have no feelings," he said.

I managed to pull myself together. "Can I get you some

coffee or something?" Some part of me needed to act like a good hostess.

He stared back as if expecting me to be in shock or something since I wasn't making much sense anyway. "I can stay for a while." He looked out the window. The crowd had dissipated but Rudy stood there watching me and Garland through the Old English lettering on the window that spelled out Troy Hardware. His expression was pinched, a man who could hardly believe what he was seeing. Garland added, "Or maybe you should go stay with a friend tonight."

"No." I raised a hand to my forehead and felt like a fool. "Really, I'll be just fine." The store was hot in comparison with outside and I wiped sweat off the sides of my nose. "I'm awful sorry. Your first full day back in town and you have to see the worst of us."

He shook his head as if to say this silliness wasn't a problem for him. Then I became aware that he was holding both my hands. Not in a romantic way but concerned and caring. The warm skin was like velvet on mine and I held to him, still not quite myself.

The doorbell jangled. Rudy came in, his embarrassment composed but with a hint of suspicion toward Garland. "Don't pay us no mind," he said. "We fight like that every day. It's our pass-time."

"Do you realize how stupid you sound?" I spat, wishing he'd shut up.

"I do," he shot back. "But it's my stupid to be."

I realized he didn't know what he was saying. He was so

mad at seeing me favoring Garland he'd say whatever wild nonsense came into his head. When I nodded toward the kitchen, he stomped off. I turned to Garland and shrugged. "I'm sorry again. He's not like this, really."

"Are you sure you'll be all right?" He kept looking beyond me as if checking out the safety of my home. "Yes," I said.

"Sure?" One of his hands touched my arm.

"I promise."

"I'm just across the street if you need anything." He turned, somewhat reluctantly. "Be careful."

I nodded and promised again that I was okay although I had to admit I was flattered by the attention, by the sense of someone caring. It sent a tingle up my spine. Something I'd never felt before. Almost like destiny was pulling me his way.

6

———

What in the world was wrong with me?

Rudy hardly spoke the rest of the evening and fell asleep in his rumpus room. I hadn't been mad at him at all. It was that stuck-up Cassandra Dimsdale's fault. She got me stirred up and I just went off. For a long time I lay in bed thinking. Me and Rudy hadn't fought this bad since the time he washed his hunting clothes with the bed sheets and tried to hide it by spraying my White Shoulders cologne on the mattress. We both smelled like sweet dead squirrel fur for six months.

Once I started to go downstairs and get Rudy but changed my mind. What could I have said to him that he'd understand? I'd acted crazy and that was all there was to it, but I sure couldn't admit it or talk about all the funny things I felt inside whenever Garland was around. Though I wasn't sure, I thought I heard Rudy on the stairs once or twice. But soon I drifted off and slept in fits. We'd never spent an entire night apart.

I got up at six a.m. to make the pomegranate pudding. Near seven he came to the kitchen and sat at the table. I asked him if he wanted breakfast, but he didn't answer.

He picked up a pomegranate and began seeding it. Then he grabbed up another, and another. For half an hour the only sound in the kitchen was his spoon scraping seeds into the mixing bowl. When he was halfway through the basket he looked up at me. "Is this enough?"

"For the first batch," I said, trying to sound friendly. "If everybody in town comes to the party then I want to have extra in the fridge."

"Good idea." He started on the rest of the pomegranates. "Your desserts usually get eaten up before any main courses."

I had my back to him but a smile spread through my whole body. Maybe the craziness was over. "Thank you, Rudy."

"I was thinking," he said. "Business is usually slow the couple days after Thanksgiving."

"Yes?"

"Why don't we shut down, go to Knoxville, take in a movie."

I blinked several times. We'd never closed the store for more than a single day since we'd been married. We'd even opened up on holidays if someone pecked on the window and needed something. "I'd like to see the art gallery at the University. Rachel said it is real interesting."

He stared at the table. Going to an art exhibition would

be like water torture for him. "Art gallery," he repeated.

"I could go by myself," I suggested. "Maybe you could go bowling or to a movie."

He got up, came behind me and slipped his arms around my waist. "I'd like to see some pretty pictures."

We held each other for a few minutes, enjoying the quiet and the familiar comfort of touch and stillness. Relief filled me up, and I guess Rudy was equally sorry for all the silliness. Then, back to work.

Around eight, I went outside and started setting up tables for the free merchandise used to get people inside. Most of the other merchants were doing the same thing. Garland had paper pilgrims standing among his vegetables, and a special table for his orchids with little place cards explaining what they were. He looked up once and waved. I nodded, grateful that he didn't come over. I needed to stay away from him for a while.

By ten o'clock, Troy was humming. People from all over the county came to our Annual Tuesday-Before-Thanksgiving Sidewalk Sale. The artists' shops on the east end of town were the most popular but the hardware store always had an opportunity to unload summer inventory. Every half hour I raffled off a bunch of garden tools and flower seeds on the promotions table. Rudy worked inside mostly, taking orders for tractor parts and carrying heavy merchandise to customer's cars. He was good at that sort of thing. But I noticed he also spent a lot of time outside with me.

"Brought you some hot chocolate." He handed me a

steaming mug and rubbed my arms. "You need another coat?"

"Naw," I said. "I'm used to it now." I should have known everything was going along too well. Jimmy Lee Novack and Owen Thelkel, two of Rudy's buds-in-crime, staggered up with goofy grins and smelling like beer. Their shirt tails were pulled out and both wore baseball caps turned backwards.

"Hey, Rudy," Jimmy Lee yelled over a handful of people inspecting the on-sale lawn furniture. "Heard you need a little help in the oogle-doogle department." He clapped one hand on his crotch and jacked it up and down.

Rudy was good at ignoring him even though his cheeks flushed a pearly pink. I shot them a look to back off but both were too drunk to care. "Come on, Rudy," Owen yelled. "What's wrong in Pecker-land? After all, you're married to Helen of Troy."

"Helen of Troy," murmured several people in the crowd. "Who's Helen of Troy?"

I figured I'd better put a stop to the intoxicated foolery before it got out of hand. "Sorry, folks," I said, picking up a long-handled, garden spade and edging over to the two drunks. "Sheriff's down at the restaurant and hasn't had time to clean out the riffraff so sometimes we have to do it ourselves." I swung the tool like a bat and knocked Owen on his butt. Jimmy Lee jumped back, his eyes wide in surprise. I leaned toward them and growled, "Get your sorry hind ends out of here before I take the backside of this shovel to the both you."

Jimmy Lee dragged Owen to his feet and they stumbled away, cackling about Helen of Troy.

Sweetly, I turned back to the customers, my best merchant's smile on my face, and gave away more promotional items. Rudy had disappeared into the store. I peered in a couple of times when he pulled more overstocked items to the front display areas. He never would look at me.

During the next half hour people started showing up asking to see Helen of Troy.

"Now that's just a fable," I said to the first couple. "But we got some electric blankets on sale that'll keep you toasty all through winter." I looked around. Rudy was on the other side of the porch. He'd heard it all and his face was like stone.

"That's Helen of Troy," one teenage girl whispered to another. "But did you hear about her husband . . .?" She leaned into her friend, covered her mouth and whispered.

I looked sideways and saw Rudy stomping toward the store, letting the door slam so hard the bell nearly fell off. He reappeared about two hours later and couldn't have picked a worse time. Marsha Dixon and Mitchell, her loud-mouthed little boy dressed in Indian garb, were looking at a plastic swimming pool Rudy had filled with water and some floating plastic frogs.

"Is it true you and the man across the street got into a fight over Helen of Troy?" Mitchell asked, staring up at Rudy.

"No, that ain't true," he said pointedly and moved away from the pool and the frogs.

"Want to borrow my bow-and-arrow to shoot him down?"

"Not today," Rudy said through gritted teeth. He shot me an irritated glance as his boot heels clomped on the sidewalk harder than he needed to walk.

I kept my eyes on him and worked my way through the crowd in his direction. Old Man Selcutty was already talking to him. "I got some hoochie-juice back at the house," he told Rudy. "My grandpappy always said it's a fine, powerful aphrodisiac."

Rudy stepped off the porch with a look of rage. The veins in his neck stood out. I held my breath. I thought he might slug Mr. Selcutty. "Rudy," I called out. "He's an old man!"

Rudy stood directly in front of him and cleared his throat before speaking. "I'd appreciate if you'd not mention that again," he said in a controlled voice. "Children are playing around and maybe it'd be best if you took it somewhere else."

I was so proud of him. He'd acted like an adult instead of kicking something. However, he didn't look over my way, seemed to deliberately avoid my direction like he was mad at me for something I didn't cause.

Several times that afternoon Cassandra passed by on the other side of the street. Her screechy voice carried like a fire siren. I went out of my way not to look in that direction and if she glanced over, I pretended not to see her. Of course, I knew better than to think she'd give us peace for one whole day. When she finally sauntered over, clipboard in hand, she was tapping the pen impatiently against it.

"Well, if it's not Helen of Troy."

I glared at her, hoping that was enough to shut her up.

"I swear I've never seen anybody get this town as stirred up as you have today."

"Pudding's ready," I said, trying to keep conversation to a minimum. "You can check it off your list,"

"One more thing I'd like to check off my list." She looked down at the clipboard, biting one side of her lips.

"What's that, Sandy?" I couldn't resist using the despised nickname.

"Just a piece of advice."

I rolled my eyes, but decided to listen with my mouth shut and get rid of her as fast as possible. If Rudy could do it, so could I.

"I don't know what the story is between you and your husband. And I don't really care to speculate on your sexual proclivities. I leave that to professionals in those fields." Her voice took on the whisper of girl-talk. "But you really ought to leave other people out of your personal problems." She paused and looked back at her brother's store. "Garland's had a difficult time this past year. It took me forever to convince him to move back here. He should be able to live without being pulled into your messes."

My teeth were biting down on my tongue. Wasn't a thing I could say back to her, and I hated admitting to myself that I agreed. I shouldn't have let Garland get so involved and I sure did owe him an apology. But somehow Cassandra standing there telling me to stay away from him was a streak of fire up my backside.

"You have a charming and sensitive brother." I kept my tone calm and even. "Thoughtfulness is a trait I've always admired in men. It's a shame it doesn't run in families."

She smiled tersely, held up her clipboard and checked something off. For a second she stared over my shoulder, then narrowed her eyes at me before stepping sideways and going on to her next checkpoint.

I turned around. Rudy stood in the doorway. His hard expression looked hurt, as if a trusted friend had stolen something from him. I hated that he'd heard me and wished I could take it back. What I'd said was aimed at Cassandra and didn't have anything to do with him. But his demeanor spoke more than that. He knew something had changed between us. And while I stood there wishing it hadn't, wishing we could ignore all the foolishness of the day, I knew that things were different. What I didn't know was what to do about it.

7

Torches blazed on each corner of the town's intersection. Wood stacked in the center for a bonfire would burn so warm nobody would have to wear a coat. It was getting to that exciting time of day. The sale was over and the party was ready to begin. All the residents came out and even a few tourists hung around for the evening festivities. The square was crowded with tables of food and drink; musicians and dancing were on the north and east sides; old-timers telling Jack-tales on the south; and ladies gossiping on the west. The streets were lined with strings of lights and I would guess that from high in the sky we looked like a big illuminated 'X.'

I carried out my bowls of pomegranate surprise and placed them on the dessert table with Mary Margaret's carrot cakes. Rudy was helping stack the bonfire. Maude stood beyond him watching both of us. She slowly ambled toward me. The closer she got, the more I saw how tired and hollow-eyed she looked.

"Honey, are you okay?" I asked.

"Let's not talk about me." She tugged my arm and led me toward a patch of trees in the park at the north end of the street. "What's all this I been hearing today?"

I sighed and put a hand to my forehead. "I don't know how it all got started." Someone had strung a clothesline between two rotting ash trees and I grabbed on to it to avoid supporting my own weight. "First Cassandra Dimsdale got going on me, then I had a fight with Rudy, he kicked down my flower box and slept in the rumpus room. I thought we'd made up but now everybody's bothering him about being married to Helen of Troy and he's mad again. How I got through this day, I'll never know."

Her eyes softened and her sweet smile had such sympathy she didn't have to speak. She looked over to one side when a whiny noise came from the bushes. "Hear that?"

I peered through some grapevines growing along a wire fence. Neither of us saw anything but the closer we got the more familiar the sound. "It's crying," I said.

When I spoke the noise stopped except for small, stifling hiccups. We picked up a mass of grapevines. Tansy sat in a hollow underneath, her face puffed up from crying, trembling like a baby bird that had fallen from its nest.

"Child, what's wrong?" Maude pulled the girl out and wrapped both arms around her.

She tried explaining but couldn't stop the sobs.

I sat on a tree stump and took Tansy in my lap, stroking

her hair and rocking her. It soothed her but she was so upset, she couldn't get a word out. We carried her back to my house and warmed a washrag to clean her face.

"I'll go find Rachel," Maude said.

"I can do that," I volunteered.

She looked back at Tansy, sitting in the rocking chair, her little hands clutched in front of her, shoulders shaking and limbs trembling. "No," Maude said. "She takes to you. Try and get her to tell you what happened. I'll be back fast as I can."

I got my brush and ran it through Tansy's hair. "You've got the most beautiful hair," I said. "The color of clover honey."

She smiled a little and looked over at me, but couldn't sustain eye contact for more than a few seconds. Her thoughts seemed to have a disturbing hold on her that went right down to the bone.

Finally, she took my hand and spoke in small gasps. "Miss Cassandra brought a special delivery letter today. Momma's friend was just leaving the trailer. Miss Cassandra said 'cause she was postmaster, she was well aware Momma got welfare and wasn't supposed to have a man living with her."

Tansy's face flushed bright red and tears drifted down her cheeks again but she tried her best to keep from sobbing. "She said . . . she said . . ." Her lips puffed with worry and she couldn't continue.

The backdoor swung open and Rachel rushed in, followed by Maude. "Oh baby, where have you been?" She hugged her daughter up into her arms. "I looked everywhere for you."

Then, as if we needed more trouble, Cassandra romped up the walk, clipboard in hand, tapping her pen on it. She took one look at what was going on and turned quickly to leave.

"Just a minute." I lunged outside and whipped around to block her. "Cassandra Dimsdale, who in tarnation do you think you are scaring a poor little girl like that?"

"There's no reason to blame me." She stuck out her lower lip in self-righteous indignation. "People make their own beds and have to take responsibility for their actions."

"He doesn't live there." Rachel stepped forward and spit her words right into Cassandra's face. "Just visiting for a few days."

"Thank goodness I do deliver the mail and can report first hand what I saw to child protective services."

Rachel looked ready to hit her. "What goes on in the privacy of my home is not the mailman's business!"

"But it is," Cassandra touted, letting her mouth curl in a cruel sneer. "When a child is being corrupted and subjected to who knows what—"

"I am not corrupted," Tansy cried, her eyes filling with tears as she wrapped her arms around Maude's waist.

"Enough!" I interjected, getting between Rachel and Cassandra. "Sandy Dimsdale, get off my property. You better never set foot on those back steps again."

She inserted the pen behind her ear, then turned. "Mark my words—"

I rushed inside and slammed the door.

Tansy had run into her mother's arms and they clutched each other. I put an arm around both of them. "Now, don't you worry, honey. Nobody is going to take you from your Momma."

Rachel wiped her daughter's cheeks, kissed her forehead, then shot me a worried look. I shook my head to indicate we didn't need to scare Tansy. But we both knew Cassandra would not go away easily. "That's right," Rachel said. "You're my lucky charm. And Helen here is witness to it."

"Okay," Tansy said tentatively; every limb of her little body still trembled.

It broke my heart. Watching that numb expression on her face, a look that wanted so much to trust, threw me back to my eight-year-old self, newly orphaned and all alone, my parents and baby sister dead in a fire I'd somehow escaped. Maude had said something to me then that I never forgot. I knelt down in front of Tansy, leaning close enough to whisper. "People here love you, and even if the gods rain down fire from heaven, we're never going to let you be alone."

Tansy nodded, so determined to be brave. One hand held mine and the other held her mother's.

"Now," I said. "We're going to the party and we're going to have the best time ever."

"Yes, we are," Rachel said, giving her daughter's hand a squeeze. "Let's go get on our party clothes. I'll even let you wear makeup tonight."

They left and I closed the door, watching them as far as

the road. Maude had sat down in the rocker and I noticed again how tired she looked. She pointed up at me, a soft smile on her face. "You remembered what I said to you all those years ago."

"Maude, I used to watch the sky for that fire, and if it'd come I would've run home to you and known you'd find a way to fix it."

She looked down at the floor. For a minute I thought she might cry. I knelt down beside her, put my head on her knees and, for a while, we just sat there. She stroked my hair and hummed but I knew more was on her mind. "Cassandra is going to be trouble," she predicted.

"What makes her like that?"

"She comes from a long line of bossy women," Maude said. "I'll always remember her sixty-eight-year-old grand-mother rallying a bunch of church ladies into shattering the windows of Ned Bailey's pool hall and breaking the cue sticks, all the while keeping every hair in place and ensuring her gardenia coat corsage didn't get mashed."

"What in the world did Ned do?"

"Sold her husband some bootleg liquor."

"That's all?"

"Not a family of women to cross."

"Even I remember her mother cursing out the choir director because Cassandra wasn't the featured singer."

"They know how to hold a grudge."

"And Sandy couldn't even carry a tune."

"A long line of bossy, know-it-all women."

"There's a bonfire out there. Can't we just tie her to the stake? End it here?"

Maude chuckled. "The gods used to punish humans who thought they knew too much. It may be we'll have to leave Cassandra to God."

8

—

Rudy was right that my pomegranate surprise was gone before anybody even started on the salads, chips or fried chicken. It made me feel good as I went back and got the extra we'd made just in case. Every now and then I'd slip a few pieces of Mary Margaret's carrot cake back to the house. She kept checking to see if anyone was eating it—nobody had taken any and I saw no reason for her feelings to be hurt.

The band was made up of Granddaddy Harold on guitar, Liz Hanson on piano and church choir members who doubled on various percussion and horn instruments as well as sang. When they played "Silver Threads and Golden Needles," some of the younger people moved out and danced. I spotted Joan Jackson, the bookmobile librarian, on the edge of the crowd and worked my way over to her. "So glad you made it," I said.

"I've been hearing so much about this, it seemed a shame

to go another year without attending." She smiled wide and pretty with a bookish intelligence that shone through sparkling gray eyes. Joan usually had her hair pulled back in a severe ponytail, wore thick glasses and hardly any makeup. Tonight her hair was down, she wore her contact lenses, and even without makeup was a nice-looking woman of about twenty-eight. Far as I knew, she had never been married.

"There's someone I want to introduce you to." I pulled her around the edge of the dancing to the side of the square where Garland manned a grill. He was flipping burgers, hotdogs and chicken wings and waved at me with the spatula. I motioned to him and pulled Joan up beside me. "Someone going to relieve you on that, I hope," I called out over the heads of some youngsters waiting for their hotdogs.

"Elmore Page'll be here in a few minutes."

"Good. I want you to meet our librarian." I turned to Joan. Even though she had a hesitant smile, her eyes were focused on Garland and she liked what she saw. I felt good about that. As long as I'd known her, she didn't seem to date much and with the lack of single men in this county there weren't a lot of pickings. She was also smarter than most men, which didn't help. Garland just might be a perfect match for her.

A few minutes later he followed us over to a bench. I did my duty and left them discussing James Agee and Walker Evans's *Let Us Now Praise Famous Men*. I admit I felt a twang of jealousy. Garland had been mine alone for his first couple days in town. But looking back, watching their spirited conversation and how they seemed so in sync with each other, I knew I'd done the right thing.

I was on my way back to check the dessert table when I heard the voice of my beloved.

"I'm a descendent of Hessian mercenaries, so plundering is in my blood." Rudy hung upside down from one of the rotting ash trees in the same park where we'd found Tansy. Both arms were stretched out, his biceps flexed like a circus strongman, a half-empty bottle of beer between his knees and a cigar hanging from the corner of his mouth.

Oh, Lord, I thought. What now!

I wriggled through the crowd, and the closer I got, the more I could see what a dangerous position he was in. He hung six feet up with a pile of empty beer bottles littering the ground underneath him. "Rudy," I called out. "Your Momma was Scottish, your Daddy was Scottish and your grandparents were Scottish. There's not a bit of German Hessian in you, so get down from that tree before you break your neck."

He flipped himself upward, spilling some of the beer and barely hanging on to the tree limb.

"Go on, Rudy." Jimmy Lee Novack sneered. "Prove you ain't so whipped."

"Jimmy Lee," I warned, grabbing him by the collar of his unbuttoned shirt. "If he gets hurt, I'll hunt you down like a dog and make you yelp."

When Rudy straddled the tree limb it cracked under his weight. He started to stand up and all I could do was hold my breath. Then, I saw the prize. Someone had tied a quart of Kentucky bourbon in the crook of two limbs, but he'd have to straighten all the way up and stand on tiptoes to reach it. Rudy drained the rest of his beer and dropped the bottle. It shattered on the pile below. He rose to his full height, waving both arms around to keep his balance, and reached for the liquor while puffing on the cigar. He could only touch the bottom with the tips of his fingers. The tree limb bent under his weight and dead bark rained down as he took another step. A gasp rippled through the crowd.

"Three have tried and three have failed. Only I will win the prize," Rudy called out. "Watch this, Helen."

I could barely breathe and closed my eyes more than once when he shimmied up to a higher and leaner branch. "Rudy, please come down."

All around me people murmured:

"Don't think much of what he's doing but I love the way he's doing it."

"Kinda makes me want to keep my knees together."

"That ranks right up there with chocolate spaghetti."

"Well, he's just not very bright, is he?"

Rudy reached one last time. Bouncing up and down on the limb and grabbing the bourbon, he landed on one foot and swayed precariously. Of course, he lost his balance, falling face forward while holding the bottle high and safe. He landed on the limb, which caught him square in the crotch, then he dropped to the ground with the wide-eyed stare of a man about to vomit.

A chorus of "Oooooos" shot out in the crowd. Rudy struggled to his feet but only got as far as a bent crouch, trying to shake off the pain. He held the bourbon above his head in triumph and spit the stump of the cigar on the ground. The crowd clapped and hooted.

Someone behind me said, "That'll take care of that premature ejaculation problem."

I ran up to him as he straightened up, hiding what must have been intense agony behind a frozen, gleeful expression to proclaim himself master of the dead ash tree.

"What in the world were you thinking?" I said, shaking him by the arm.

"I won this." He twisted off the top and took a swig out of the bottle amid a round of applause.

Leland Jarvis spit some tobacco juice then slapped him on the back. "Just like the crusades," he said, offering a chew to Rudy. "They didn't learn very much but they had a damn good story to tell afterwards."

"You almost broke your neck for a bottle of liquor," I fussed.

"Kentucky bourbon," he replied.

I could smell enough beer on his breath to know he had impaired judgment even before he climbed that tree. "Stick to beer, Rudy. It's cheaper and you get the same effect."

He glared at me, probably upset that I was not congratulating him like the rest of his buddies. "Well, Helen," he said, holding out the bottle and looking back at a half dozen of his good ol' boys. "It's the difference between a high-priced call girl and an old slut who just wants to spread her legs and lay there."

Another "Ooooo" went through the crowd.

I tucked in my dignity, reeled around and stormed away. No use talking to him when he's like this. If he was going to show his tail, he'd have to do it without me. At the back of the crowd, Cassandra stood like a disapproving mother. She stared at me and shook her head. I would have kept on walking but the prissy roll of her eyes demanded a response. "Well," I defended him, "he did win."

"He's got Furies in his bloodstream," Cassandra said. "Can't never be satisfied with plain, happy life, always has to prove hisself."

"Sandy," I said. "Pick up your elephant nose before it gets stepped on for sniffing in other people's business."

"Tell me, Helen of Troy, what do you need with a short, bald man who smokes cigars and has a problem with premature ejaculation?"

"I think Rudy has plenty of hair," Rachel said from behind us.

I couldn't have asked for better revenge. Rachel stood there, all five foot nine of her, in a clingy red dress that looked like it had shrunk in the dryer. Her boobs nearly spilled out the top and a slit on the side gave her long legs plenty of walking room. Cassandra's mouth dropped open, then her eyes narrowed with a take-no-prisoners look.

"Rachel," I said, "you look stunning."

"A little visitor from child protective services came by.

Had to fill out some forms before I came here." She dabbed the edge of her mouth with her pinky finger.

"Next time I'll advise they send a woman." Cassandra's lips trembled as if biting back words a lady wouldn't say.

"Your war paint's a little smeared, Sandy." Rachel tossed her hair. "Oh, there's your husband. Think I'll go over and tell Archie hello."

Cassandra looked like she might explode. I dipped my head and shook it, trying to indicate to Rachel that maybe she was going too far.

Cassandra stepped right into her face. "Didn't your parents ever instill you with any sense of morals?"

"They tried, but it's kind of like fractions. I didn't want to learn fractions in fourth grade and I don't want to learn how to be a dried-up hag now." She stepped around Cassandra, swishing her hips more than necessary and grabbing a beer from the ice chest with one sweep of her hand.

"Don't worry, Sandy," I said, turning away myself. "Archie's the humdrum type. No Furies in his blood."

I went to the quiet side of the street, sat on a bench and glanced at Rachel several times. That dress was a might much, but it did have the desired effect. She'd taken Roland Carter by the hand and was dancing with him. At least he's single, I thought, and a little too old for her taste. She was still a sight to see and more than a few women pulled their men away.

Rachel downed the beer then wiped her mouth with the back of her hand without missing a dance step. She exchanged Roland for Clyde Leonard and, after a few minutes, Jerry Dwyer had joined the pack, waiting to be her partner.

"Everything going wrong just fine?" I heard Garland's voice behind me.

"Well, sit down," I said, indicating the seat beside me. "You having a good time?"

"The best." He sat and leaned back to look up at the stars then over to me.

"Where's Joan?"

"Had to get home, something about the bookmobile's rounds starting at six a.m."

"She's a nice girl."

"Promised to bring me some books on orchids." He looked upward again and pointed at the full moon about to come up high in the background of the party. "I think I'm liking it here."

"Good." I patted his arm. Off to the side I saw Rudy guzzling his bourbon. He and his buddies were around their own smaller bonfire in the park, passing the bottle like it was bounty from a hard fought battle. Garland noticed but was kind enough to pretend he didn't. "Would you like to dance?" I asked, wanting to get my mind off what I knew was going to be a fight when I got home that night.

Garland stood and held out his hand. I took it and led him toward the dancers. Instantly we joined in, bobbing and stepping to the fast rhythms of "Can't Hurry Love." He could hold his own with the young people and twice a circle formed around us as he dipped and spun me. Several of them clapped and whooped with enthusiasm. Finally, out of breath, I motioned I had to take a rest.

"One more," he said, pulling me into his arms as the band played a slow introduction to "A Kiss To Build A Dream On." He had a happy smile on his face and seemed to let go of some of the sadness that weighed on him.

I put my arms around his neck, trying not to breath too heavily. "You're such a good dancer," I said. "You're going to be one of the most popular men around." He smiled and pulled me closer, and I rested my head against his shoulder and closed my eyes. I felt like I was melting in a warm liquid in a place that was too comfortable to move.

As we slowly spun around I looked out at the crowd and saw Tansy waving at me, all dressed up in last year's Easter outfit, a yellow dress with embroidered white daisies. Her makeup was subtle enough that she looked like a little lady. I waved back and she smiled. In the next turn she'd been replaced by Cassandra, scowling like a bird at a scarecrow. For meanness, I pulled Garland a little closer. The sleepy dance held my body like a brace. Winded as I was, I felt like I was standing on a moving carousal, half dizzy, not able to focus on one single person except my own thrill of being traveled around and around. I thought I saw Maude and then Rudy. They looked at me with concerned expressions, but I was too dreamy and this dance made me happy. When the music stopped, part of me wished it hadn't.

"I was worried about coming to this tonight," Garland

said. "I'm not very sociable."

"You did just fine." I rubbed his arm as we walked toward the outer circle of the party.

"Because of you," he said. Garland leaned down and kissed my hand. "I feel welcome."

"You are." I touched his cheek and recalled looking up into his eyes when he was an eighteen-year-old boy. I knew then what he'd made me feel back when I was a scared little girl. He made me feel safe. Garland had fought fire, then conquered and destroyed it. In a lot of ways safety was what I'd looked for my entire life. A place where I could rest and no one expected anything of me. A haven that could never burn down. I don't know why his touch gave that to me. "Be careful," I said, not sure he heard me. I wondered, was I saying those words to myself?

His wide back shifted as he walked toward his store, looking around several times, a happy smile on his face, a contented sway to his pace. Whatever events had haunted him, he seemed to have let go of those memories. I hoped so, for his sake. He deserved to be a happy man.

The crowd had begun to thin and Tansy ran up to me, giggly and sleepy-eyed. "I've had the best time, Helen."

"I'm so glad," I said. "Did you get some pomegranate pudding?"

"Two helpings."

"Let's go find your Momma and get you home to bed, tousle-head."

We walked around the food tables and circled through

the dance square but didn't see her. I avoided the second bonfire that Rudy and his buddies had made. It seemed better to keep Tansy away. I could pitch my fit tomorrow when Rudy had a hangover and couldn't fight back. They'd clipped up a sheet with clothespins, probably to hide their drinking from the children. I didn't see Rudy. Most of the men were lined up on a log, glancing back and forth at each other and the thinning crowd. Sheepish is the word that popped in my head.

"Come on, Tansy," I said, "Let's check the other side." I looked back at the men. Something seemed wrong. They passed the bottle of bourbon that Rudy had won. No talk. They appeared to be waiting.

"Yonder's her purse," Tansy said, pointing at a tree stump half hidden by the sheet. She ran toward it.

"Tansy, come back!" A flash of what was happening sprang in my head like an evil vision.

She pulled the sheet aside and half the clips came undone at her tug. Her mother was behind it, in a clutch, kissing someone. The man's hand was on her breast, her bare leg slipped from the slit in the skirt and wrapped around his.

"Momma?" Tansy said. "What are you doing?"

I hurried forward and pulled her back. The men scattered. The music stopped and it seemed the only sound was the muttering of people whose attention had all turned toward this side of the party.

"Oh, God," Rachel said. The man's face was still buried in her neck. She pushed him away.

I thought I was frozen or struck dead. Rudy looked up at me. His face flushed as our eyes locked into each other's. He wiped his mouth with the back of his hand and stared at the ground.

"Rachel, what the hell are you doing?"

"Don't be mad," she said.

"You walked in here with your dress up over your head and your legs spread, and you're surprised I'm mad?"

She avoided my eyes, one hand on her forehead another smoothing her skirt. "It was only a kiss."

"With my husband." I shoved one of her shoulders.

She stepped forward, defensive, reeking of alcohol. "Well, Helen of Troy, if you knew how to please a man—"

"I'm sure you can please them but you sure as hell can't hold them."

Tansy tugged at her mother's dress, crying. "Momma, please, please don't fight with Helen. Momma, why're you doing this?"

Rachel froze. She stared at her daughter, growing aware of her surroundings, coming to herself, realizing what she had done. "I'm sorry, Helen." Tears fell down her cheeks and she pressed a hand to her face. "Sometimes I hate myself." She turned and ran, breaking through the crowd. Tansy followed her into the darkness.

When I turned around Rudy had disappeared. Figures, I thought, just like him to hide out. The men who'd been lined up for their turn at Rachel now scuffed their feet against the ground and stared different directions.

"You-all thought you were about to get a show." I ripped down the rest of the sheet and threw it at Kent Buford. It caught him square in the face and he brushed it aside but didn't say anything. "Thought you'd see a catty girl-fight." I shoved Rufus Dillard and he and several other men shuffled away.

Rudy is here somewhere, I thought. Looking into the dark woods I could sense him and stepped up to the tree line. "Come out and face me!" Seconds passed. No answer, only the blue darkness of the woods. The ache that filled my heart pulsed through my veins to every muscle in my body. "You hide in your shame!"

When I turned around the one person I didn't need to see stood there with her arms crossed and her mouth twisted in a sarcastic smirk.

Cassandra took one step toward me, pursing her lips. "Uh-huh, now you don't have such a big mouth on you, do you, Helen Ramsey? Now you know how it feels to have your husband in that woman's arms. Just like I've been telling you all this time."

I picked up the bottle of bourbon and emptied what was left over Cassandra Dimsdale's head.

9

———

The night turned from chilly to frosty as I walked home but I couldn't feel the cold. My blood stewed, heating my skin with a thin film of perspiration. As I approached the back entrance a figure next to the door stepped forward but remained in the shadows. Rudy, I thought, half hoping. At the same time my insides knotted with injury and longing. Then the person stepped into a blade of moonlight and I recognized Maude Fletcher. I'd never seen her as mad as she looked standing on my back porch, arms crossed, eyes dark as storm clouds.

"'Bout time you got home," she said.

"Did you see what he did?" I asked, expecting her to rally to my defense.

"I saw you acting bad as a roughneck at a rooster fight."

For a few seconds I sweated like a delinquent under a schoolteacher's glare but after catching my husband kissing another woman and a good friend at that, I wasn't about to accept being called the bully. "Most women would be looking for a lawyer right now."

Maude stepped down to my level and looked me directly in the eyes. "That what you want?"

All the venom froze in my veins. I looked down at the chipped sidewalk with dandelion spouts pushing through the cracks. What I wanted was a question that had never entered my mind. All I'd thought about was my own fury. The time had come to decide how to deal with both of them. Rudy and Rachel.

Maude took my hand, leading me to the steps, where we sat between two terracotta lions Rudy'd won for me at the county fair. With one finger she lifted my sulking chin. "How much of this has to do with Garland Cookson?" she asked.

I shook my head ferociously but somehow words of defense wouldn't come out of my mouth.

"I saw how you danced with him," Maude said.

"No," I managed to blurt, then went into a defensive mode. "For goodness sakes, I introduced him to Joan Jackson." My hands fluttered as I explained and I couldn't hold them still. Maude noticed and her lips flattened into a steel line. I looked away, unable to bear her stare. "Those two will be dating in no time," I added, then forced myself to face her. She must believe that I had had the best of intentions.

Maude tapped a foot, deliberately blinking her eyes at the same time. She clasped both hands across her knees and nodded toward a rose bush growing beside the gate. Its thorny branches were November bare and entwined the fence lattice. "Remember when you planted that?" she asked, but continued without me responding. "You picked the flowers of your marriage bouquet from those vines. Said every time you left by that gate, the roses would remind you of where home was."

"It's not me that got off the path."

"Really?" She looked over at the grocery store. "I'm going to tell you something Rudy would never want you to know."

"Rudy keep a secret?" I let out a laugh. "You know him. Everybody's best friend. He can talk carburetors with the garage mechanic and hair gel with the beauty shop girls. By the time he's done he'll know their life stories enough to defend their weaknesses to the preacher, and explain to the tax man why he should go easy on them."

"He kept a secret from you. One he still lives with." She leaned forward and stared up at the stars. "Before you got married, Rudy came to see me. He was afraid."

"Second thoughts about the wedding?"

"He didn't want you to live a life less than what you could have with somebody else. Somebody Rudy thought might be better for you."

I shook my head. "What do you mean?"

"Andrew Riordan."

"Andrew. . . ." A lump formed in my throat and doubled in size. I hadn't spoken that name since senior year in high school. Now, I saw our state congressman on TV occasionally or heard his radio speeches. Senator Riordan, a politician with a twinkle in his eye and a way of passing through town and drawing every living voter to his cause.

"What did you tell Rudy?"

"To fight for what he wanted his life to be, because that's all any person could be expected to do."

My mind spun and I rested my forehead into my hands. "Maude, he went out and punched Andrew, gave him a black eye. How could you let that happen? It's lucky Rudy didn't end up in jail."

"Ahh," she said and waved a hand. "It probably got ole Andy a few votes. He's got no reason to complain."

"Nothing ever happened between us. He was an older, attractive man back then. Twenty-five if I remember. He asked me to work on his campaign. I was flattered." Maude's sideways glance told me she wasn't buying it. "He turned my head," I admitted, "but just for a minute. That's all."

"Garland's got that same fishing line floating in the water."

"What am I? A trout? Some doll to be paraded around, long as I don't think or feel? I claim no special powers. How can I rise above what ordinary folks pass off as a mistake, a moment of weakness to be forgiven and then it's on to the next day? It's the nights I can hardly stand. An emptiness haunts me, Maude."

She jerked me toward her. "People see how special you are. They sense the good fortune you could bring to their lives, whether it's a politician looking for the right kind of wife or a lonely man wanting to be saved."

82

"I don't know if I can let him go." I covered my face with both hands. Those words burned in my mouth but I knew they were true. Part of me was already lost in a delirium of the attention Garland had heaped on me. "Maude, help me."

She released her grip and looked up at the moon, a white plate with a broken edge, then let out a slow, measured breath. "I don't think I can."

I slid down a step and wrapped my arms around her legs. She stroked my hair, patted my shoulder and rubbed my shivering arms. "He looks at me and I feel everything I used to feel with Rudy."

"Girl, you're afflicted with a fever that even the strongest ice can't break. If I can offer any kind of advice, it's for you and Rudy to leave this town tonight and not return 'til you've found what you love in each other again. Once you've craved the forbidden, you suffer until that appetite is satisfied. But then, it may be too late to save your marriage."

I looked up at her, hoping her face would show answers. "Maybe this life together isn't worth working at anymore."

"I'll tell you what I told Rudy all those years ago: decide what you want before circumstance decides for you."

I gazed into the backyard, watching as a fleet of moonbows began their journey across the enclosure like sailing ships. In a few nights the moon would lose its light until next month. "Where do you think Rudy is now?"

"Up in the tree house." She motioned toward the tall beech tree at the far corner of the back lot. "His momma told me he always went there when he was in trouble."

A chuckle escaped my throat. "Only place she couldn't catch him to whip him." I stood, walked into the yard and studied the darkness in the tree limbs but could see nothing. "You think he's watching us now?"

She didn't reply. I reached out my arms among the dancing moonbows, letting the colors shine on my skin, then turned toward the roof of the grocery. If Rudy wasn't looking down at me, Garland was definitely watching my backyard. From where I stood he couldn't see me but his classic profile and patient stance were clear. It was hard to imagine what he might be thinking. Maude slowly pushed herself up, the joints of her knees cracking. She followed my line of sight then cupped my cheek, her soft palm smelling of vanilla.

As she walked away she glanced back before closing the gate. So many times she'd been there at what I always believed was my darkest hour but this time she had no answers for me.

I went inside and looked out through the kitchen window. Garland was no longer peering down from his roof. He'd been waiting on me, I realized. Probably fighting some of the same feelings as mine. Was this unspoken attraction so different from what Rudy had done when he kissed Rachel? I closed my eyes, wishing I could take back this day. I longed for sleep, hoping my dreams would bring relief. Tomorrow I had a husband to deal with and a former friend to put in line. Like Rudy, I'd fight for what I wanted my life to be. For better or worse, this marriage was mine and I had to find a way to make it work. If only I could settle the unrest in my heart.

10

An insistent rapping at the front door woke me up. I looked at the clock. Seven a.m. I'd overslept. Grabbing a robe, I hurried downstairs, maneuvering around leftover merchandise. It was still dark outside but I could see lights from the grocery store as Garland accepted a delivery from a meat truck. Then panic set in as I realized who stood on our front porch: Paxton Crow, the county sheriff.

He so seldom came to Troy that when we did see him it was nearly always on account of bad news. Had someone reported Rudy for public drunkenness? Every year a few men got plastered and this year was no exception. I unlocked the door and invited the sheriff inside. He removed his hat, showing white hair combed back with his scalp showing through. Crow nodded and looked down at the floor.

"Sheriff?" I said. My stomach twisted like I'd eaten something bad and all of a sudden it occurred to me. "Maude?"

Sheriff Crow shook his head. "No," he said, still hesitant. "Rachel Kincaid and her little girl were in a car accident. The child's in the hospital at LaFollette and one of my deputies has taken Maude over there. She asked that I come by and tell you, uh, so you'd know where she was."

"Oh, Lord, is Tansy okay?"

"Broken arm looks to be the most serious injury but doctors want to keep her for observation until they're sure."

I leaned against the counter, anxiety surging through my veins. "Rachel was loaded as a coal truck last night. What in the world possessed her to get in a car, and with Tansy?"

Crow blinked several times, passing his hat from one hand to the other. "The car plunged over the mountain at Hell's Point Ridge. Took us several hours to even get to them."

I couldn't look at him. Something else was wrong. I squeezed my hands and felt the nails dig into my skin. "What is it?"

"Rachel, uh, she didn't make it, Helen. She died at the scene." He scuffed his feet on the floor, nervous as anybody having to deliver that kind of news. "Maude wanted me to tell you that she'd be by as soon as she could."

I nodded my head, unable to speak. He put on his hat and I walked him to the door and watched as his police cruiser stirred up a flurry of snow that had lightly coated the ground. Behind me came a noise of someone moving and I figured Rudy had come in during the night. In the window glass I saw his reflection staring at me. He must have heard 'cause he bowed his head as if saying a prayer. He didn't speak or move toward me, just stared at the floor, waiting for me to turn around. As my body woke up it seemed that for the last few minutes I'd forgotten about last night. Now it all came back, surging through my body like a rip tide. I couldn't believe Rachel was dead. Just couldn't. Poor little Tansy.

"Want some coffee?" Rudy stepped forward and asked.

I opened the door and walked outside in my robe. I needed fresh air. Cold as it was, the iciness brought me to a reality that I wanted so much to disbelieve. The town square was a mess of tables, boxes, trash, the smoldering bonfire still bright with orange embers despite the snow. In an hour or so volunteers for cleanup would make everything look just like it did yesterday. But now wasn't yesterday. Our world had changed. Rachel Kincaid was dead. I could see Garland inside his store, unpacking the early delivery. Holding tightly to the post that anchored one end of what was left of my flower box was all that kept me from walking over there.

Word of Rachel's death swept quickly through town. By midday almost everybody stopped by the store to say a few words. Everyone except Cassandra, who at least had the good sense to hide in her post office. If not for her, I don't think Rachel would have gotten so crazy last night. That was what bothered me, I guess. I'd said some pretty ugly things myself. I kept re-living the night in my head. So many things could have been different.

The shopkeeper's bell rang and Garland came in holding a miniature yellow orchid in his hands. "Thought this might brighten your day," he said, placing it on the counter in front of me.

"That's so sweet." I reached over and rubbed his forearm. "It has been a hard day."

"I'm so sorry about . . ." He paused, looking at me directly. His slate-colored pupils were large and dark.

I nodded my head, for the first time feeling tears rise up to my eyes, and, embarrassed, quickly wiped them away. Garland reached across the counter and put an arm around me. I felt silly being unable to control myself, and except for Maude, he seemed to be the only person I could accept sincere sympathy from. "Thank you," I said as I pulled back.

He took a handkerchief from his pocket and gave it to me. "Terrible for her little girl."

The sound of throat clearing came from the stockroom. Rudy stood in the doorway, his expression confused but his eyes aiming beads of irritation at Garland. He sauntered to the front, his gait like a gunslinger. "What's this?" he asked, touching the rim of the flowerpot.

"A gift," I replied, not about to take any nonsense from him.

"A flower," Rudy said, touching a petal. He shot Garland another glare and picked it up, balancing it in his hand like he was weighing a melon.

Garland took back the flowerpot and placed it on the

counter, sliding it toward me. "Come on over to the store if you feel like talking." He glanced at Rudy, nodded, then turned to leave.

"In most towns," Rudy said with the tone of an announcement, "men don't usually give flowers to other men's wives."

"Rudy," I scolded.

Garland stopped right in his tracks. He turned his head just enough to give Rudy an offended look without having to inconveniently adjust his own stance. "In most towns, men remember who they're married to." He straightened up like a warrior and reached deliberately for the door handle. "Good day, Helen."

"I'll be talking to you, Garland," I called after him, then gave Rudy a look that I hope rattled him right down to his toes.

"Now, Helen, I know what you're about to say." He held his hands out in front of him like they'd help him explain. "You saw how she was dressed. The only man in this whole town who didn't get a hard-on was Noley Gates, and he's half blind."

"Rudy, did you ever think . . . did you ever once use your little pea brain and think that maybe she was just a lonely woman who wanted somebody to love her?" I came around the counter and stood in front of him, shaking my finger in his face. "No, you didn't. You were too busy letting Mr. Weasel do the thinking for you."

"It's not like I knew this was going to happen." He swallowed, looking away, remorse blushing his cheeks.

"I know that," I said, fighting my own guilty feelings. "None of us did." I took off my work apron and tossed it on the counter. "Watch the store for a while. I'm going to make myself some warm water."

He turned but didn't follow me. "Why do you always drink warm water?"

"Because that's what I drink when I'm upset!" My attitude shut him up. He'd probably expected worse but I was too worried about Tansy to give it to him right now.

Just as the water started to bubble, Maude tapped at the back door. I snatched it open and we fell into each other's arms, then held on so long it was hard to break apart. The wheezing kettle interrupted us.

"How's Tansy?" I asked as we sat at the kitchen table.

"Her body will heal. But she's so tore up about her mother."

I wiped my eyes and pressed hard on the aching pain in my temples. "Lord, if we could just think far enough into the future to see what damage our actions do. What in the world was Rachel thinking?"

Maude hesitated and looked aside. "She was leaving town."

"What?" My whole body felt frozen, just like when I saw Rachel and Rudy kissing.

"Her car was packed to the ceiling with their belongings."

"Because of me!" My hand flew to cover my mouth.

"You don't know that." Maude rubbed my arm, trying to assure me. "It could just as well have been Cassandra's threats. People from social services are already at the hospital getting ready to put Tansy into state custody."

"Well," I announced with authority, "they can't do that." I'm not sure what I meant but the words came from so deep inside of me they sounded right. It was almost like Tansy was part of our landscape and to have her taken away was something that couldn't happen. "Didn't Rachel have relatives?"

Maude shook her head. "Maybe a second cousin in Montana. The police are trying to locate him now."

"I can't believe this."

"Helen," Maude's voice softened but was determined and as serious as I'd ever heard. "I want you to adopt Tansy."

For several seconds I couldn't speak. I looked at her, then away, then back at her large, doe eyes. They were firm and didn't leave mine. "I, I don't know," I stammered. "I don't think I could."

"She loves you," Maude said.

"And I love her. But I don't know anything about kids. I've never had any."

"She needs you. That's all you need to know. It's all I knew."

"Maude, you should do it. When the state officials know your background, they'll give her to you."

"No," she said, a sadness edging up into her voice. "No, they won't."

"But you raised me. And a whole handful of kids were in and out of our house growing up. They've all done well. You turned them all around."

"My illness—"

"No." I pressed my fingers to her lips. I didn't want to hear this.

"My time's too short." She shook her head and took my hand. "They won't give her to me."

Her peaceful features implied she had accepted her fate with gentleness, contentment and recognition all rolled into one. Part of me wanted to say no, tell the world this couldn't happen, that we'd had enough change in our town for one day and needed to rest. Maude just shook her head. No one could argue against Death.

In those few seconds, it was as if her strength entered me. After she left I sat for a long time staring out the window at the changing leaves, whose colors seemed to have faded to brown overnight. Now we were left with snow flurries that melted as soon as they touched down, leaving the ground a dark, muddy mess. No one could predict the twists and turns of life, right now so tragic. The world might have been a blizzard around us, but here in Troy we just lived on and took care of each other. One way or another, we kept going. Maude knew the value of taking one day at a time and she'd made a difference in this town and in the lives of more children than I could count. Now, it was my turn.

I went to the front of the store. Rudy had the newspaper spread out in front of him on the counter. "Rudy, I need to talk to you."

He looked up but not at me. His mouth slightly parted and his pale blue eyes blinked several times. He came around the counter and stopped directly in front of me. "You're going to ask for a divorce, aren't you?"

"What?" My mind was still on Maude's request, and it took me a few seconds to realize he was really worried. "No, Rudy. I don't want a divorce."

He fell to his knees in front of me, wrapping his arms around my legs so tight I nearly lost my balance. "Thank you, Jesus," he said, "'cause I don't know what I'd do without you."

"Rudy, let me go." I tried to step back but he clung to me all the tighter and I had to grab the counter to keep from falling. He mumbled something unrecognizable into my skirt. "Rudy, I need to ask you for something."

"I sure have learned from this," he said, staring up into my face.

I uncrossed his arms and forced him to stand. He looked deeply into my eyes like I was a princess and he could deny me nothing. "I want to adopt Tansy."

"Honey?" he gasped, turning away, digesting my request. "Tansy's a half-grown kid."

"She's a little girl who's going to need somebody."

"Got relatives, don't she?"

"Maybe." I circled around him, my muscles tightened in resentment at his hesitation but trying to understand it. "That's not the point. I want her and she needs me, us."

"Where would she sleep?"

"How 'bout that rumpus room?"

"In there?" He pointed toward the stockroom that led to

his precious lounge. "With my pool table and tool chest? In Myrtle's room?"

"Why are you fighting me on this?"

"Honey," he said again as if not knowing how to respond.

"Don't *honey* me."

"Why can't we just have our own kids."

"Ooooooo," I let out a frustrated growl. "Our own kids? And where would they sleep, in that dilapidated tree house?"

"It's not the same."

"Why? Because she's Rachel's child?"

"I'm sorry for what happened to Rachel, but that doesn't mean I should be responsible for her child."

"Well, you sure seemed to care what happened to Rachel when you had your tongue halfway down her throat!"

"I can't argue about this now," he said and turned away from me.

"Well, we have to decide; the people from the state are going to make a decision about her."

"Can't Maude take her? She took you."

Something like a flash of lightning struck in front of my eyes. Suddenly I saw me and Tansy, the throw-away kids. It was like my whole childhood came to life before me. Rudy was just another bothered adult who didn't care what happened to us. Tansy and me were just the same. Always dependent on what people gave us. Never had a thing of our own. Little runts that people like Rudy sometimes took pity on if in the long run it'd benefit him. My arm swung out in a wide arc, walloping him right across the back.

"Damn, woman! What'd you do that for?"

"You ignorant, self-absorbed redneck."

"That's uncalled for."

I picked up a fan and threw it at him. "You shallow, empty-headed, self-centered jerk!"

"Helen," he said, his voice turning serious like he was about to scold a child. "Put down that frying pan!"

I flung it, breaking a twelve-inch hole in the front window, and the pan went sailing out into the street. "My entire life I've been taking care of you, your family store, entertained your brothers and their silly city wives when they came to visit, tended your mother as she lay dying, scrubbed and mopped and worked when I was sick as a dog! I never asked for nothing. You know the reason I never asked?"

He barely got out the word "No," 'cause I threw a tin garbage can at him. It crashed on the floor making a racket like a cat chasing a mouse through a pottery shop. He held out one hand like a stop sign. I threw a glass pitcher and barely missed his head. "You hear me?" he shouted. "I said stop this!"

"I never asked for nothing 'cause I thought I didn't deserve it. I thought I was lucky when people offered me any sort of kindness. I thought I owned nothing in this world and even the stuff in our rooms wasn't mine. I was an orphan even in this marriage, depending on your good graces for the food I ate."

"Now, Helen." His face had a pained look of trying to reason with me.

I threw a hatchet and it stuck in the doorframe beside his face. "A person shouldn't have to feel that way!" I yelled. "A person shouldn't have to spend their whole life being grateful." I let loose a bunch of cuss words. I knew I was out of control and didn't care. A bunch of townsfolk had gathered outside the window and were looking in at us. Rudy waved his arms, trying to shoo them away. Just as he turned back toward me, someone broke through the crowd and the door slammed open, the bell dinging wildly.

Garland surveyed the broken merchandise and the torn apart store. "Are you all right, Helen?"

I nodded, half-coming to my senses. What in the world had I done? Before I could explain, he shoved Rudy backwards, causing him to fall over a picnic bench and land in the toddler's swimming pool. Water splashed and plastic frogs flew up into the air. Then, Garland scooped me up in his arms and carried me out the door.

11

————

I felt like I was trapped in a whirlwind. Crowds of faces whipped past me as we crossed the street. A jumble of hands. Arms flaying. Being hoisted into the grocery store. I fought the sensation of being whipped by on a Ferris wheel where I couldn't hold to any one image. Garland lowered me into a chair beside a warm potbelly stove in the front left portion of the store where people sometimes gathered to play chess. Then he ran back to the door, locked it and pulled the shade over the window. He peeked out toward the street before coming over to me.

"I won't let him hurt you."

I stood up, still a mess of confusion. "Rudy won't hurt me."

"Helen," he said sternly to get my attention. "Look at yourself."

He turned me toward a mirror. My hair was a mass of tangles, tears I didn't even know I cried had puffed out my eyes and cheeks and I'd bitten my lip so hard that it bled. "Rudy didn't do this."

He ran back to the door to see if anyone had followed us over. Sure enough some of the men and boys who usually gathered at Hootie Keefer's diner for the $5.25 dinner special were crowding around the front windows where there were no shades. Others were still across the street standing with Rudy. My husband held out his arms, dripping wet, and Patti Mills from the beauty shop came out with some towels to help him dry off.

"Get away from here!" Garland yelled at the spectators. They hissed and giggled, shading their eyes as they stared in at us.

"I've got to get back over there."

"No," he said firmly. "I won't allow it. I won't sit by while a man does this to a woman even if she is his wife."

"Garland, honestly. I'm okay. If anything Rudy got the worst of it."

Both his hands cupped my cheeks. His gaze penetrated into my eyes and his seriousness held my attention. "I've seen this before. You can't admit what's happening to you. I sat by last time and did nothing. I'll never do that again."

With one arm he pulled me back and sat me in a rocker beside the potbellied stove. He leaned behind me and before I could say anything he wrapped me twice with a rope and tied the ends in a knot.

"You can't do this," I said.

"I can and I have," Garland asserted. "If you can't see

what's good for you, you'll have to wait it out here until you do."

Outside Rudy's voice came thundering. "Garland Cookson! I got no fight with you but you bring my wife out here to me right now!"

Garland went to the back of the store and returned with a rifle.

"Good Lord, no!" I cried out. "Rudy ain't done nothing to you."

"I can't believe you're defending him."

"He didn't do anything to me either, really. I did all this. I started the fight, a quarrel over adopting Tansy."

"You go on back home, Rudy," Garland shouted out the door. "I'm not letting Helen out of here until I know you've calmed down."

"Well, we'll sure as hell see about that."

From the side window I could see Rudy charging the store. When he couldn't open the door, he banged against it. The wood shook and the windows rattled like they might shatter. Garland stood on a barrel, aimed the rifle out an airshaft and fired into the air. At the blast sound all the men scattered.

"That man's crazy," someone yelled.

"He ain't crazy," another voice insisted. "He's protecting the woman he loves."

I groaned and strained against the ropes. How did I cause such a mess?

"Somebody go get his sister," a woman's voice shouted.

"Yeah, get Cassandra!"

"No!" I yelled. "Not that. Anything but—"

"I'm calling the law," Rudy said. "He's kidnapped my wife."

The next several minutes were quiet. I didn't dare move as Garland went from window to window, stacking produce tables so no one could see inside. He held on to the rifle and I kept my eye on it. He must have noticed cause finally he put it down on the counter and knelt down beside me. "I'll untie you but you have to promise me not to go back over there."

"I promise." I said it softly, hoping fear wasn't coming out in my voice.

Just as the ropes fell away the door handle jiggled. Garland rushed for the rifle but I ran faster and got between him and it. "No," I said, holding out my hand against his chest. "No violence." He tried to reach around me and we tussled for the space. Of course I couldn't know that whoever was on the other side of the door might not have a gun too and I held my breath when a key went in the lock and the door pushed open. We both went stone-still.

Cassandra stood there. She had on her postmaster uniform and thick glasses that made her eyes seem three times bigger. She slowly looked around the store at the knocked-over cartons, toppled can goods, vegetables laying on the floor. A Granny Smith apple rolled past her feet and out into the street. She stepped inside, eyes on her brother. "Have you lost your mind?"

Garland and I looked at each other, frozen in an awkward scuffle, the rifle still wedged behind me. "No," we both said at the same time.

She shut the door, came to us and wedged her hands in between our chests, pushing us apart. "Are you holding this woman against her will?"

"No," we both said again.

She looked from one to the other of us, then turned, letting her hands fly out to the side and slap her thighs. "I, I, I guess I'm the only one who's confused." She whipped around like lightning. "You got to send this woman home!"

"I will not," Garland spoke.

"Well, finally, one voice." Cassandra wrenched her head like she couldn't believe what was happening. "Then you just go," she said to me.

My feet rooted to the floor, even as my mind told me to hightail it home.

"Helen's not going anywhere." Garland stood in front of me. "Her husband was hurting her and she's staying here."

He looked over at me but I didn't know what to say.

A small breath caught in Cassandra's throat for several seconds, then she burst out laughing. "Rudy and Helen have fought like roosters for as long as they've lived in this town. For godsakes, she bloodied his nose on their wedding day."

"That was an accident," I said.

"I was there, I saw it," Cassandra shot back.

I looked at Garland, wanted to explain. "I was feeding him the wedding cake and accidentally . . . oh, why am I explaining this to you, either of you. I have to go home to my husband."

"Perfect!" Cassandra said.

"I'll go when I'm good and ready," I said, turning on her like the rooster she'd called me.

"You're not going at all," Garland said. "Helen, stay the night and think this through."

I stood in the center of the room, looking at the mess of collard greens scattered on the floor. He hadn't meant any harm, just misunderstood what was happening. I had to make him see the mistake. "Garland," I said softly, pulling one of his arms to get him out of Cassandra's earshot. "I know you thought you did the right thing and maybe you did but this really was a disagreement between me and Rudy and we've got to solve it."

"I know what I saw." He opened both his palms and then took my hands. "I couldn't stand it if I stood by and let someone hurt you."

"He won't. I've been married to him a long time and we quarrel and fuss but he's never raised a hand to me."

He stared into my eyes, as sympathetic a look as I had ever seen from a man. It was as if he looked right down into my insides, trying to figure out what made me work. I had to admit I admired him for it. How many times does a man ever try and understand?

A tap on the door. "It's Sheriff Crow. Can I come in, Mr. Cookson?"

"Now see what's happened." Cassandra moved to open

the door. "Of course, Sheriff. Come right on inside, out of the cold, the snow."

I looked past him out toward the street. A light snow had begun. Rudy stood on the edge of the sidewalk trying to see what was going on inside. He'd obviously been told to wait there by the sheriff but his agitated shifting back and forth showed that wasn't going to last long. Several people around him were patting his shoulders, trying to keep him calm. He'd changed into dry clothes but the ends of his hair were still wet and pasted against his neck. As the door closed on him all I could think was he was going to catch cold.

"Mrs. Dimsdale, Mr. Cookson," he nodded toward each of them. "Mrs. Ramsey."

"This is all a terrible mistake," Cassandra said. "I'm sorry you were called."

He looked straight at me. "Mrs. Ramsey, are you all right?"

"Yes—"

"Of course she is," Cassandra interrupted "and she was just going home."

"Helen." Garland turned toward me. "Don't do this."

"Are you being held against your will?" the sheriff asked.

"Of course not," I answered. I would not get Garland in trouble. He'd had the best of intentions and this was a misunderstanding.

Rudy stumbled through the door, appearing to have been pushed by some of his friends. "That's my wife and I want her home!"

"Shut up," I whispered toward him.

"Sheriff," Garland said, "surely you can see that this man thinks he owns this woman."

"She is his wife," Cassandra hissed toward her brother.

"She is not his property." Garland slammed his hand down on the counter. "Sheriff, take a look at that hardware store. There's merchandise thrown around, a broken window, turned-over cabinets. Can you in good conscience send this woman back in there?"

The sheriff glanced around at the disorder of the grocery store and gave Garland such a peculiar look that his cheeks flushed. "Look, everybody here is an adult. So where are you sleeping tonight, Mrs. Ramsey?"

"Well, bless, damn, with me," Rudy hollered.

"Of course she is," Cassandra said.

"So let's get going," Rudy continued.

"Okay." Cassandra opened the door and a whisk of snow blew in. It mixed with the heat of a coal fire in the potbelly stove and a bit of steam hissed in the air.

"I'm staying here," I said, hardly believing I said the words.

"What?" Rudy and Cassandra said at the same time.

"If Mr. Cookson will allow me to use his spare room then I'd like to stay here, at least for tonight."

"Fine," the sheriff said. "Subject closed."

"She can't do that!" Rudy pointed at me as the sheriff pushed him toward the door and he mouthed my name but didn't say it.

"She can." Sheriff Crow gave Rudy a final shove.

"Helen?" He stared at me like a lost puppy. "Tomorrow's Thanksgiving."

I was so confused I didn't know what to say.

The door closed and I could hear the sheriff lecturing Rudy not to come over here again tonight or he'd be thrown in jail for trespassing. I started toward the door, then stopped. What was I doing?

"Brother," Cassandra said. "Suffer the consequences of your good deeds." She glared at me, turned with a huff and slammed the door behind her.

Suddenly the quiet seemed to close in on me. A moan came up through my throat and I covered my mouth with both hands. What had I done? I wanted to run outside, run across the street, but I couldn't. I just couldn't. And I didn't know why. Garland put his arms around me and I cried.

12

I sipped a cup of warm tea then stared into the golden water. Garland moved around the store picking up knocked-over tables, sweeping up ruined vegetables and fruits that lay scattered on the floor. He was meticulous in putting things back together like a puzzle, stacking canned goods into perfect pyramids, and layering collard greens and spinach into symmetrical blankets of green between beds of rosy red radishes and pumpkin-colored sweet potatoes. He moistened the veggies with a light spritz of water until they glistened. His touch and eye for detail reminded me of a caring father dressing a child. Part of me couldn't help contrasting how Rudy unloaded our merchandise, hauling it into the stock room like so much junk then dragging it out piecemeal when we had an empty shelf and shoehorning it in wherever it would fit. I was always the one who attended to the presentation. Garland saw me watching him and smiled. He seemed so calm after everything that had happened.

"I won't be much longer," he said. "I need to duct tape this counter so it'll hold together."

"No hurry." I got up and walked toward the back of the store where a butcher block was covered with corn meal. I smoothed the grains, then used one finger to write the words *hold together*. What would have held Rudy and me together? What would have kept him from kissing another woman? Me from staying here? Rachel from getting into that car? It seemed everything that had happened was a misstep that could have been prevented. On a wall calendar a picture of a dozen cherub angels looked down on me. A baby, I thought. If we'd had a child maybe none of this would have happened.

I leaned against the butcher block, wiping out the words. It's not that Rudy and I didn't discuss having a baby early in our marriage. He'd always say *"if it happens, it happens."* But we never exactly planned for it. We made love often enough but I'd never gotten pregnant. As I got older we just stopped talking about it. Most women push for having a child, but I never did. I wondered why my body didn't give me the longing that most women have. Was I just afraid?

I jumped at a scratching on the back door. "Rudy?" I said. I looked toward the front of the store. Garland set aside a broom and hurried over, his face registering disappointment I couldn't dismiss. He'd heard me call Rudy's name.

Looking out the window, both directions. No one there. He turned back toward me and shrugged his shoulders. The scratching started again. Garland looked out and down. When he opened the door Myrtle sauntered in, headed straight to a multi-colored rag rug tucked in the corner, and curled in a circle like a frequently invited guest.

"Myrtle?" I knelt beside him and stroked his head.

"That's Myrtle?" Garland put one hand to his stomach and chuckled.

"Our dog."

Garland opened the freezer, walked in and returned with a tin bucket that had MYRTLE painted on it in red letters. "I wondered who this was for." The beagle jumped up and licked his chops. Garland poured hot water on chicken gizzards and livers then emptied them into a yellow bowl beside the rug, and Myrtle chomped down.

"No wonder he only eats half the food we put out for him," I said.

"Looks like he kept my daddy company. Now it makes sense that he told me I could change anything I wanted about the store, but leave the rag rug right where it was."

I sat in a straight back chair beside the door, imagining old Mr. Cookson and his relationship with my dog. He must have been a lonely old man, but none of us ever realized it. "Myrtle's fat as a little pig now," I said. "When we were looking over the litter, he was the runt."

"Gave him a fightin' name."

"Myrtle was my idea," I said, a trace of embarrassment warming my cheeks. "Same name as a doll I lost as a little girl. We were supposed to get a female puppy but Rudy felt sorry for the runt, so tiny he fit in the palm of my hand."

Garland scratched the beagle behind the ears until Myrtle

had eaten his fill. Then the beagle plodded over to the door, turned and looked at us in what must have been a familiar routine. "Well, Myrtle, you're welcome back any time."

I watched out the window while my dog trotted toward the hardware store, figuring he'd dug a hole somewhere under the rear fence. From there he could slip into the rumpus room through a crack in the wall that Rudy had always been meaning to plaster.

"See, Helen," Garland said as he closed the door. "Part of your life was already here and you didn't even know it."

He touched my shoulder. I told myself to move away, but couldn't. Turning slowly, I laid my hand on his and said, "I think I'd like to get some sleep now." He didn't object, and stepped back, being gracious.

When I was alone in the spare bedroom, I remembered the day me and Rudy brought Myrtle home. We couldn't stop playing with the tiny beagle. Half our work didn't get done and finally the puppy dropped from exhaustion. For hours afterward we were so filled with energy that we stayed up half the night, making love again and again. Rudy could hardly stand leaving my side back then. We'd spend whole afternoons kissing, and if there were no customers we'd make a game of necking in every part of the store. Recalling those days brought one terrible thought to mind. I realized why I'd never gotten pregnant. It was a hateful, selfish reason and I was ashamed to admit it. I didn't have a baby because Rudy adored me and I didn't want to share him.

13

——

I spent most of the next morning sitting beside the pot-belly stove, staring at the fire as if it were a crystal ball that might give me answers. All I got were confusing images of flames shooting up like jagged pieces of glass. I moved the chair back a foot. Garland put in a big piece of coal around nine a.m. and closed the stove door. He cleaned up around me and put a sweater over my shoulders. I didn't speak, only sat there, thinking, not sure what came next. Around noon I had to do something. Across the store I spotted a plump holiday bird, and asked, "Is that turkey on the meat counter for supper?"

He nodded.

"You call your sister and her husband and tell them Thanksgiving dinner will be ready around six."

He nodded again, this time with a slight smile.

I carried the bird to the upstairs kitchen but before starting on it went to the front bedroom and looked outside.

Below, Rudy stood just inside the door of our store, watching Garland's grocery. Except for pouted lips his face was flat, eyes unblinking, a fixed, stubborn expression I'd gotten used to through the years. I salted the turkey and rubbed it with butter before packing it with cranberry maple almond stuffing, then I couldn't help but check on Rudy again. He had not moved. Six times while that turkey baked I peered down and he stood there like a guard. No telling what was going on in his head.

Garland brought up some potatoes for mashing, green beans and frozen corn, and then set the table with his special pink-flowered china. "Cassandra's bringing some rolls and a chocolate cake," he said.

I nodded, getting out the potato peeler when it suddenly hit me. I was about to have Thanksgiving dinner with the nastiest woman in town while my husband was sitting across the street all alone. Garland went to take a shower. I rushed to the front of the store and put one hand on the doorknob, ready to leave, and with the other, I raised the window shade. Rudy and I looked at each other. Our eyes locked like children facing each other in a game of Red Rover, Red Rover, I Dare You Come Over. I knew then why I would stay. I had something to say to him. I just didn't have the words yet and until I did I couldn't be in the same room with my husband. My thoughts seemed to find their way across the street because he broke his stance, turned around and left my sight. I went back to cooking a meal that I doubted I'd be able to eat.

"Some of my mother's dresses are in the spare room closet," Garland said, coming into the kitchen. "They're not quite in style but I believe they'll fit you."

"When Maude gets back I'll have her get some of my clothes."

I took my turn in the bathroom, stood a long time under a hot shower, then picked out a navy dress with tiny red roses sewn around the hem. It fit fine but when I stepped back into the dining room Cassandra's hard-featured glare made me realize I'd made a mistake.

"That was my mother's best Easter dress," she said, holding a pan of rolls from the oven and dropping them onto the table. "She usually wore it to funerals."

My feet felt stuck in mud and my lungs were inhaling smoke. "I can go change," I said, my cheeks warming as I turned.

"Nonsense," Garland told his sister. "Helen doesn't have anything and this will do for now."

Cassandra glared more intensely and pushed her six-year-old son, Herbie, up to the table. We all took our seats. No one remembered to say grace. Her husband, Archie, sat across from me smiling politely and trying to ease my discomfort. Garland began slicing the turkey and talking about changes he had in mind for the store. His sister's pinched face focused on me until Herbie spit out a mouthful of green beans and she turned to clean him up. I'd never felt more unwanted in my entire life. By the time we cut the chocolate cake, Cassandra's face was pinking up and I knew it wouldn't be long before she issued one of her predictions.

"Supposed to be a storm headed this way." Her gaze flitted toward the window, taking in the dark sky.

"Were the streets slick when you drove over?" Garland asked Archie.

"No more than usual." He took a bite of cake and made an "mmmmm" sound.

"I've cranked up the generator in the greenhouse," Garland said. "Hard to duplicate the rainforest in the middle of a snowstorm, but if you get too cold in your house, come on over here."

"Where would we sleep?" Cassandra looked directly at me.

I laid down my fork, chewing the cake that tasted like chalk in my mouth.

"There's room," Garland said. "I'll turn the living room into a campsite. You'd like that, wouldn't you, Herbie?" He tousled the boy's blond hair.

"I will not have my son subjected to—"

Archie stood up quickly and patted Garland on the back. "You've done fine things with the store."

Cassandra leaned in close to me. "If you won't go home, go to Maude's house."

"She's still in LaFollette with Tansy."

"Then her house is empty."

"I will not break and enter. I'm fine here."

"It is not fine here," she hissed. "It's a travesty."

"If you hadn't started up with Rachel, none of this

would've happened."

"That was not my fault."

"Look at what you've done to poor Tansy. Would you want that for your own son?"

"My son is being raised in a Christian home."

Cassandra and I had stood and faced each other across the table. "You never over worry about logic, do you?"

"Ladies!" Garland said, rising along with us.

Cassandra ignored her brother. "And you? Miss Sweetness-and-Nice kneeling at the Savior's cross?"

"I've reevaluated my life over the last couple hours and have come to realize that in the entirety of my years, every day, every hour, every minute, I should have been a bigger bitch!"

She gasped, her mouth dropped wide, and she turned toward her son and clapped both hands over his ears. Herbie twisted his small head up toward her, frowned and pointed at the cake. "Mammma!"

"Let the boy eat his dessert," Archie said.

"Arch, we're going home!"

They might have left except for the clamor of glass shattering in the downstairs store. For seconds we all froze in place. Then all eyes focused on me.

"You women stay here," Garland said. He and Archie took off down the steps.

"I just bet this has to do with you." Cassandra pulled her son to her.

I went halfway down the stairs and looked into the store.

Garland and Archie stood in the dark, watching the road. In the middle of the floor was a brick, trailed by shattered glass from one of the door panes. The street outside was covered with a thin layer of snow and three sets of footprints down the middle. I heard laughing and moved behind Garland.

The tracks led to Rudy, Jimmy Lee Novack and Owen Thelkel. They held to each other in a crunch, snickering and pointing, not even trying to hide what they'd done, and all three of them so drunk they could barely stand. Rudy stepped forward and shook his fist. "Garland Cookson," he shouted. "You are lower than a snake's belly." All three burst out laughing.

"Go on, tell him, Rudy," Jimmy Lee encouraged.

"What'da I do next?" Rudy swayed backwards, still laughing and trying to keep his balance.

"Do rat's toes."

"Yeah, rat's toes."

"Garland Cookson," Rudy yelled. "You are lower than rat's toes!"

"Let me handle this," I said, and pulled back the curtain from the broken pane. "Rudy, you're gonna catch your death out there. Go on home to bed."

He stood straight and stared at the store. "Well, I guess you're all cozy in bed yourself!"

Several lights went on from the apartments over the stores. Garland stood behind me, his hands on my shoulders.

"There's no need for you to talk like that," I said to Rudy, then focused on the other two. "Jimmy Lee, Owen, you got him drunk, now you take him home and stay with him 'til he sobers up. Make sure he's covered up and turn the heat on; I don't want the pipes freezing if it gets too cold tonight."

Owen turned sideways and threw up. Jimmy Lee and Rudy began giggling like hyenas. "Tell you what I'll do," Rudy called out, his limbs swaying so badly he looked made of rubber. "I'll swap you a flower box for a wife."

"You're a waste of a man," Garland shouted.

"Tell you one more thing. I wouldn't waste my spit on you much less my breath. So you want to stay, Helen of Troy, then you stay, 'cause you're no longer welcome in my home!"

"That's a'tellin' her." Rudy's friends clapped him on the back and they all stumbled on down the street.

"Yeahs!" came from the apartments where people had crowded at their windows to see what was going on.

"Shut up, stupid!" someone else hollered.

The three of them didn't go into the hardware store and I kept them in sight until they disappeared around a corner. I turned away from the cold breeze that was blowing steadily, my arms wrapped around my waist.

"It's the liquor talking," Archie said. "He won't even remember it in the morning."

"I will." I went back upstairs and curled up on the bed in the spare room. Seconds later Garland knocked. I said I was okay, but I wasn't. I lay there trembling, not knowing what was going to happen to me.

14

———

I remember someone saying that a man should never make a woman cry because God always counts her tears. I wiped my cheeks and held in a trembling breath. Cassandra and Archie had left without a word. For a while there was quiet, then the tinkling of glass. Garland must be sweeping up. I wanted to go down and help him but each time I tried to leave the room a shivering sob rose up in my throat. I leaned against the window and watched the hardware store. All the rooms were dark. Rudy still wasn't home.

I paced from wall to wall and the same questions buzzed in my head over and over. What should I do? Should I go home? Go to Maude's? Stay here? I could hear Garland whistling in the kitchen and the clanging of pots and pans. I knew I should go in and help but how was I going to face him after bringing all this trouble into his home? He whistled "My Old Kentucky Home," then switched to "Swanee

River." Such happy tunes seemed odd when I was sitting in here worrying myself sick.

On a chest of drawers several pictures in silver frames were lined across the top. I picked one up and stared at a photo of Garland. He must have been six or seven, dark hair that fell in bangs across his forehead. He straddled a bike, smiling with no front teeth and pointed up toward a tree branch. Cassandra, a toddler, held on to the handlebars as if trying to hold him back and steal her big brother's moment in the sun.

Replacing it among black-and-white photos of his parents, grandparents and other relatives I realized that this was something I didn't have—a family history. Except for some of the older people in town who'd known my ancestors, I pretty much began with me. I had no pictures, only a family Bible with names written in faded ink. My parents were a hazy memory, almost a dream, but I had feelings of what our home had been, warm, clean and smelling of cinnamon. Now that I thought about it, being a child before my parents died might have been the only time when I ever felt truly safe. Anywhere else I went I'd made myself a place by being courteous and helpful. And now, it was time to play that part again. I steeled myself and went to the kitchen. Garland was washing dishes. Gently I edged him aside with my hips and sank my hands into the warm, sudsy water. "I've ruined your family holiday."

Garland shrugged and picked up a towel to dry. "If you could have seen some of the fights around that table through the years, you wouldn't say that."

"But I should know better than to challenge Cassandra."

Garland let out a chuckle. He pulled my hands out of the water and dried them as he led me to a chair and sat opposite. "My sister started it. My philosophy is, when you commence something you better be prepared for the consequences, even if it's getting knocked on your butt by the most beautiful woman in town."

A flush warmed my cheeks and I stumbled over my words. "But, but she's still your blood."

"Feuds have been fought over less and I'm on your side."

"Still, I hope you'll accept my apology."

"Only if you'll promise me not to worry another minute over this. Cassandra has always had a hard time understanding that people have to live their lives despite all the glorious complications and messes and confusion."

His eyes were gentle as a doe's and I could see the curious face of the little boy from the picture upstairs. "I'm sure she's been there for you during difficult times."

He looked away briefly then back at me and didn't blink for several seconds. "Guess that's what kin is supposed to do whether they like the job or not." He sat erect, a faraway expression that tried hard to hide an intense emotion I couldn't quite read.

"Why didn't you ever marry?"

"I was about to ask why you never had children."

We both looked away. "Terrible questions," I said. "What in the world's wrong with us?" I started to get up but he pulled me back down.

"They're questions that people ask when they want to touch the deepest part of the other person." He held on to my hands. "I'm flattered that you'd want to know me that well."

I nodded, embarrassment filling me and matching the warmth of our joined palms. I didn't know what to say.

"We'll finish cleaning the rest of this in the morning."

We ambled slowly toward the bedrooms. The floor creaked with our steps and a stream of icy air flowed down the hall. He caressed my back softly as I paused in front of the door to the spare room. I didn't dare look back. My heart pounded like hands were thumping a drum. He moved on. When he reached his own bedroom both of us looked at each other. Our eyes connected and seemed to braid the air between us. "In the morning," I said and gently eased open my door.

"A new day."

I entered and leaned against the closed door. Wooly emotions wound through my muscles like vines. My entire life I thought I would love only Rudy. I didn't think I'd ever have feelings for anybody beyond a movie star crush. But Garland Cookson did something to me that I didn't understand. He wasn't as handsome as my husband, as muscular or as witty but he made me feel cherished. For the first time I knew that it was possible to love more than one person. I wasn't sure how comfortable I was with that information, but now that I'd admitted it to myself, I realized how dangerous that knowledge could be.

The clock read midnight. It had been almost an hour since I'd even thought of Rudy and that was more disturbing to me than any of Garland's words. Another old saying I'd heard since I was a young girl rang in my memory. Place your shoes in a corner positioned like a T and your true love will come calling. I arranged my shoes and looked at the door, wondering who would call.

15

The next morning I couldn't keep my eyes off the hardware store. When a customer finally went inside around eleven fifteen I sighed in relief. At least Rudy had gotten home and the business was operating. I busied myself making turkey salad and cleaning up from the day before. Garland was downstairs early, but there were so few customers he spent most of the day on the roof in the greenhouse tending his orchids. I think it was our way of avoiding each other.

Cassandra came by at lunchtime and I heard them having another argument about me. I thought it best not to make an appearance, so stayed upstairs. The poor man had hardly been in his apartment at all. Maybe he was giving me time to myself but I feared he was uncomfortable in his own home.

From the living room, I looked out the window onto our store. Another layer of snow dusted the roof and the blustery gray skies threatened to storm. Then, our bedroom light flipped off and I could tell someone stood there watching me. I jerked back behind the curtain. Was it Rudy? Of course it is, silly, I said to myself. He's the only one over there. Checking on his wife. A little shiver went through me, a sprinkling of hope. But his mean words from last night still rang in my head, and although he owed me an apology, I wondered if there was anything to save.

"Helen," Garland called from the staircase. "You have some visitors."

I started down warily, then galloped two steps at a time when I saw Maude and Tansy. Tansy's arm was in a cast, held by a scarf against her chest. I pressed her gently to me and invited them over to the chairs surrounding the warm potbelly stove. While we got settled Maude seemed to notice how at home I was and whispered behind the little girl's back. "A lot going on here."

I shook my head to indicate we couldn't discuss it and focused on Tansy. "You look like you're going to get up and turn cartwheels."

"Might take me a while," she giggled, then looked oddly at me. "We wanted to get back home before the storm hit."

"Tansy's going to stay with me until a good family is found," Maude said, stroking the back of her head.

"Why are you over here and not with Rudy?" Tansy asked.

I swallowed and looked away. Garland, bless his heart, stepped in to cover my embarrassment. "You ladies look like some hot chocolate would finish off the day. How 'bout you help me make it?" He pointed to Tansy and indicated the kitchen upstairs.

She followed Garland and I turned to Maude and begged, "Please let me come stay with you."

"How did all this happen?" Maude demanded.

I put a hand to my forehead and explained as best I could. Maude listened with patience and understanding as I tried to explain the craziness of the last few days. "I can't put Garland to more trouble," I whispered, "and I've got nowhere else to go."

Maude gently shook her head. "The state people think they'll have a family in the next couple weeks. Tansy feels real guilty about what happened between you and her mother."

"And you think me being there will remind her of that."

"I need to be with her alone for a little while, the way I was with you in the beginning." Maude stroked my arm, her eyes shifting back and forth in thought. "If she was going to stay with us it'd be different, but she may be sent far away. We might never see her again. This child needs to learn she's as good as everybody else, and needs to learn it before I lose her forever."

"I'm sorry I couldn't make things work out."

"Well, I never expected it to break up your marriage."

"It's not just that kiss and the fight about adopting Tansy."

"Then what?"

"Lot of things. Rudy thinks he's in charge of the whole world. He won't listen. He's just not happy and it makes him mean."

"And you're so even-tempered."

"Maude," I said, a little shocked by her sarcasm.

"Better get to work, Helen of Troy, or you just might lose it all."

"What do you mean?"

"I mean I brought Tansy up here 'cause I knew the storm would snow her in and we'd keep her for a while longer, but she's not the only one snowed in." I twirled my hand for her to explain further. "Joan Jackson," she said.

"The librarian?"

"Bookmobile broke down at the edge of town and there's no way to get it down the mountain 'til the storm passes."

She looked at me real hard and I knew she meant more but I was afraid to ask.

"Joan's staying in Rudy's rumpus room," Maude confirmed. "It was the only spare bed in town to put her in."

"Can't she stay with some of the girls from the beauty shop?"

"Loretta's mother and sister's in town."

"What about John and Jeniece Johnson?"

"With all those kids?"

"Cassandra Dimsdale's got that big house."

"And three postal workers who can't get down the mountain."

"You?"

"I've got Tansy and you on the way."

"She might be able to stay here with Garland. I'll ask."

"I wouldn't." Maude looked at me pointedly. "You might

get the answer that she's real comfortable where she is."

Footsteps sounded on the stairs and Garland carried a tray of mugs, his expression concerned. I felt sure he'd heard some of what we had said. Tansy followed him, holding a lavender orchard. "I promise to take good care of it," she was telling him as they returned to the group. "I have a present, too, for Helen," Tansy announced

"For me?" I was baffled. "But Christmas is a month off."

Maude helped her bring in a large, flat rectangle neatly packaged in white butcher paper. I pulled off strings and the wrapping then gasped. It was a painting of me—dark brown eyes staring off into the distance, blond hair floating out from my head as if I were a mermaid underwater. The strands that flowed around behind me became Rudy's blond hair. His face was above mine, looking down on me like a protecting god. His sky-blue eyes and handsome features conjured up memories of the mountains in springtime. We were connected like flower and stem. No way to look at one of us without inevitably being led to the other. "It's beautiful."

"Momma stayed up all night painting it. We were going to have it shipped to you before . . ." Tansy swallowed and looked down. "She didn't mean what she did, Helen."

I wrapped my arm around her, squeezing her gently as she cried into my shoulder. "I know, baby." She hugged me back with her one free arm, clinging like she never wanted to let go. "I have an idea. Why don't you take this to Maude's house and in a day or two, I'll come out and stay with you."

Tansy looked at me oddly and wiped her cheeks with her one good hand. "I hope the snow stays forever so I never have to leave."

Garland chuckled and patted her on the back. "We'll live on snow cream and hot chocolate."

Tansy took a deep breath and nodded her head. "Momma always said chocolate made life worth living."

"I remember her saying exactly that," Maude said and stroked the little girl's hair to comfort her. "And how about we get some Oreos to take home with us." Maude looked over to Garland. "I'll take some batteries and candles as well while I'm here," Maude said, looking out at the weather. "It might be a long haul."

"I loaded up on them," Garland answered.

As he got Maude's items I looked outside at the street. Tansy came up beside me and held my hand. She studied the hardware store, then glanced up at me. I couldn't bring myself to explain any more than I had, and I sure didn't want to add any more upset to the poor child's life. Another half inch of snow had fallen and the flurries whipped around in a strong wind; beautiful and also savage, as wild as the thought already eating at my insides: Joan Jackson was across the street in my house with my husband. I didn't like that. Didn't like it one bit.

16

The snow fell fast and furious. Large cottony flakes came down like rain. The heat of car engines kept the streets clear most of the afternoon as people came in to stock up on supplies. I helped Garland in the store during the busiest times and, when I could, peeked over to see how Rudy was doing across the street. A few times I saw Joan carrying bags to customers' cars so it seemed she was doing the same as me. More than a few people who shopped both places commented on finding me at Garland's.

"My Lord," Loretta Gerdau said, laying down an over-sized snow shovel and a five-pound bag of salt. "It's true. You've dumped Rudy for the grocery man."

"Loretta, don't go around saying that," I warned, bagging her cans of tomato soup.

"I don't have a dog in this fight, honey. I just like to keep things straight."

I looked down at the bag of salt. "How are things over there?"

"Just like here." With a squirrelly, closed-mouth grin Loretta glanced toward Garland standing behind the meat counter, then back at me.

I took her by the arm and pulled her behind a stand of canned vegetables so other customers couldn't listen. "You know what I mean." Nosy Gladys Pickles leaned into the counter, knocking over some jars of baby food. "Gas medicine is on the shelf against the wall, Gladys," I said to her and she scuttled away.

Loretta bit her lower lip and her eyes narrowed, plastering me up and down with a you-ought-to-have-known-better look. "About half the town thinks Rudy's been asking for a good whupping ever since he tore down the town sign bringing that bulldozer up the mountain to widen his driveway. The other half is of the mind that people shouldn't interfere in a man's problems with his wife."

"What's going on over there with Joan?"

"Miss Brains got the cookbook out and last I saw was whipping up some beef stroganoff."

"Making herself useful at least."

"It smelled real good."

"Thank you, Loretta." I shoved the bag of soup toward her. My mind blanked. Rudy was eating beef stroganoff. The man had lived on fried chicken, popcorn and his favorite burnt baloney sandwiches most his life, and here he was being spoiled with gourmet food.

Loretta left and Marg Spilker, an eighty-year-old retired librarian, struggled forward with an armload of donuts, cookies and candies.

"I'll help you with that," I said. "First, let's put it in smaller bags so we can carry it to the car easier."

"My freezer and cupboard is full but I'm a little light on sweets."

"This should keep you going." I bagged it, rang it up and grabbed my coat to go out to her car. After she paid, I waved at Garland to indicate what I'd be doing and picked up Marg's bags.

Mrs. Spilker still drove a maroon 1953 Buick Roadmaster that was built more like a tank than a car. She'd taken up two perpendicular parking spaces across the street from the hardware store. Good, I thought, it'd give me a chance to look inside. I held onto her arm as we headed into a wind. Snow blustered around us and we clutched our scarves to our throats. After getting her into the driver's seat, I placed the bags in back. She turned the ignition only to get an exhausted sputter.

"My battery's dead." She looked up at me, wide-eyed and fearful.

"Wait here." I ran into the diner. A dozen or so people ate supper while a few teenagers played pool in back. "Can somebody give Marg a hand? Her car won't start."

Oren Radley and his two sons came out with me and hooked up the jumper cables. While they worked I sneaked a peek at Troy Hardware. The few people inside were stocking up on salt, shovels and giant flashlights. I could see Rudy at the register but no sign of Joan. The clanking sound of tire chains swished through sludgy snow as Marg backed into the middle of the intersection. The engine died. After several more tries, it was obvious from the weak grinding sounds that her Buick was not going to start. Rudy and Joan watched from the front window as other cars slowly moved around us. Garland came out to offer help. He tried turning the ignition while Marg sat in the passenger seat.

"You either need to buy a new battery," Oren told her, "or a new car."

"Battery's only three years old," she said, pointing at the hood of her prized vehicle.

"We have them at the hardware store," I said. Garland's head jerked toward me. I hadn't meant to startle him and his eyes narrowed as if betrayed. I looked away and told one of Oren's sons to run over and tell Rudy to bring a car battery.

A few minutes later the boy and Rudy came out together. It was the first time we'd been this close to each other since before Thanksgiving, and I felt myself shivering from more than the cold. I couldn't look at him as he came up next to me and leaned down to talk to Mrs. Spilker. He spoke loudly over a humming wind. "Told you last year I can't get parts for this car anymore, Marg. It's not your battery, it's the generator and the solenoid."

Her hands shook as she got out and stood in the snow beside her elephant of a car with its precious load of sweets in the back.

"Let me take you home," Oren said. "We'll figure out what to do about your Buick after the storm."

"But it's in the middle of the street!" Her hands fluttered to indicate its massiveness.

"I'd try to push it into a parking space," Oren said, "but . . . it's a tank of a car."

"I'll keep an eye on it," Rudy volunteered.

"So will I," Garland said.

The two men exchanged a glare.

"Everybody can drive around it. Don't you worry," I said, directing Oren's sons to help with her groceries.

As soon as that was decided, I shut the driver's door. Rudy slammed the rear door on the other side. I looked that direction and gave him the once-over, real hard. He was eating one of Marg's Hershey candy bars. When he came around front to slam down the hood I called out, "Rudy, I have something to say to you." I marched toward the trunk and waited. Garland had helped Marg into Oren's car, and as it drove away he turned to look at the two of us.

"I'm here," Rudy said flatly as snowflakes settled in his blond hair. "Say it."

"I hear you're getting some good cooking."

"The best."

"You look well-fed." My hand made a print in the inch or so of snow on the car trunk, and I stared at it as falling flakes drifted around me.

He took a step toward me, his eyes beaming. "I've never been happier."

Before I could stop myself, I swished an armful of snow right into his face. He spit, wiped his eyes and threw a handful of snow back at me. I scooped more off the car fender and heaved it at him. In seconds we were hollering at each other and throwing whatever snow we could snatch up.

Garland grabbed Rudy from behind and pulled him back. Seeing who it was, Rudy gave him a shove. They both slipped and I grabbed Garland to break his fall. The diner, grocery and hardware store emptied out, as well as the beauty shop and several other retail stores. People gathered round us slipping and sliding in pools of slush. We were a gang of disorganized ants, yelling and holding onto each other while swinging and ducking at the same time.

"Leave her alone," Loretta hollered at Rudy. "You had your chance and you chose beef stroganoff!"

"A man oughta be able to talk to his wife if he wants," Billy Kirk shouted at her. Others joined in.

"He don't own her like a slave!"

"But Garland's an outsider. Rudy's one of us!"

"He is not an outsider. He was born and raised in Troy!"

"It's Helen that's caused all this!"

Joan Jackson rushed outside and pulled Rudy toward the store. I grabbed her arm, jerked her away from him and demanded, "Don't you have any better sense than to get stuck in a snowstorm on the mountain?"

"It wasn't my fault," she tried to explain. A snowball struck her square in the side of the head and knocked her down.

Seconds later one hit me and I fell like a rock. Some of the teenagers from the diner had taken sides over Marg Spilker's car, and worked like miners making snowballs and hurling them at each other. Rudy and Joan took refuge behind a gang led by Allen Gerdau, a retired telephone repairman. Garland pulled me toward the grocery store and we ducked behind Elaine Brown's pack. Elaine helped harvest fifty acres of tobacco on a yearly basis and had biceps the size of my thighs.

"Helen of Troy belongs to us!" Allen yelled. "You give her back and we'll call it off!"

"Never!" Elaine raised her head over the Roadmaster, punching a fist in the air like an Amazon. "Helen goes where she wants and it ain't with Rudy!"

The assault of snowballs intensified, no longer a game. Adults, teenagers and some children skidded and fell, losing their hats and eyeglasses. Not even the whirling lights and police sirens of Sheriff Crow's jeep and three other deputies stopped the action. He jumped out, slammed his door and huffed over. "I got a warehouse on fire in Pruden, a collapsed roof in Eagan and a pregnant woman to get to the hospital." He strode in a diagonal across the town's intersection. "By morning, no one'll be able to get up or down this mountain, so I'm telling everybody now. Grow up!"

We all stood there looking at our feet. Snow lit on our shoulders and our breath huffed out like dragon steam. Sheriff Crow looked around. "Okay," he said. "I want Helen of Troy's people on this side."

"Sheriff, please don't call me that." I rubbed my forehead and closed my eyes.

"Rudy's people over here." As everyone moved, Sheriff Crow made sure no one was seriously injured. Garland had a bruise on his forehead and several people limped after stumbling on the salted road, but no one needed medical attention. "Now," he demanded. "I want every firearm in town in the back of my car. Now."

"Sheriff, you have no right to take our guns." Garland stepped forward, towering over the rest.

Several other men yelled, "Yeah!"

"That may be the law of the land," Crow said, "but tonight, everybody is in Troy, Tennessee and if you don't like the law the way I make it, then take me to the Supreme Court when the sun's shining." He walked a circle around us. "And don't nobody think about cheatin' the devil 'cause I sign your hunting licenses."

Over the next hour every household and store on the four streets surrendered their rifles, sports pistols, hunting knifes and home protection devices, including a few baseball bats only used for baseball. "I'll take care of the real emergencies now," the sheriff called out. "Won't be back 'til after the storm. Try not to snowball each other to death."

The three patrol vehicles and Crow's jeep drove off in different directions. All of us stood around Marg Spilker's Buick that looked like a huge maroon eggplant quickly being covered with snow. We were wet, sticky and miserable. Slowly all the townsfolk returned to the diner, the beauty shop and the other places they'd started from. I stepped up on the sidewalk and looked at Joan anchoring an arm underneath Rudy's. They went into the hardware store, closing the door behind them.

Garland touched my shoulder, but I couldn't follow him just yet. I waited until I could no longer see Rudy. Then Garland pulled me along and I went with him. Sometimes when your heart is breaking, that's the only thing you can do.

17

———

Garland led me upstairs to a couch in front of a fireplace. Embers smoldered from the night before. He threw in some wood, a newspaper and two chunks of coal. Before long, he had a warm blaze. I got up and stood behind the couch, too nervous to be that close to flame.

He brought a blanket and wrapped it around me. "You've got to get out of those freezing clothes." He sounded concerned.

"You're sopping wet, too," I replied.

He dried me as best he could, shaking my hair and blotting the dampness. "Here's a robe. Put it on while I get out of these."

I looked down. Both of us stood in a puddle. When he left the room I let my clothes drop and pulled the plush floor-length robe around me, then stepped closer to the warmth of the fire but not into its heat. "Rudy doesn't love me anymore." I suddenly realized that as if a teacher had made me write it on a chalkboard a hundred times. I would never be able to return to the hardware store, to the apartment or my bed, the kitchen or my Appalachian rocker. That life was over.

Garland returned wearing a terrycloth robe with a hood. He sat me down on the couch and with one hand drew my chin closer to him. When he looked deeply into my eyes I felt my vision glazing over and couldn't focus on anything. I turned my face again toward the flames.

"This scar," I said, holding up my left hand and pointing to a whitish triangle that ran the length of my index finger. "I burned it in a fire."

He traced the raised white skin with the tip of his thumb and enclosed my whole hand with his, holding it in his lap. "It's more than a scar."

"I was eight years old, playing with birthday candles. Lighting one, then another. Letting blue wax mix with pink and finally I held one 'til it burned down to the end and caught my fingers. I dropped it."

"Kids do that kind of thing."

"The floorboards caught fire . . . this wispy blue flame."

Garland sat up straight, studying me as he listened.

"I was barefoot. Couldn't stamp it out. I watched the silent blue turn orange, and leap up the rose-print wallpaper and onto a pair of lemon-colored curtains made from an old sheet. If I hollered for Momma and Daddy, I'd be in so much trouble."

"Helen? What happened?" He stroked the back of my head.

"If I'd only done the right thing." I stood up, clasping the robe close and shivering from the memories. "Daddy snatched me up along with our family Bible and rushed out of the house, leaving me in a cornfield, then he went back . . . he went back to get Momma and my baby sister."

The ghosts of my family seemed to dance before my eyes, awakening the trauma that defined my youth. "The old two-story house was east of High Cliff on Route 25W. When I last saw it the brown and gray boards had no color at all except for orange flames dancing in the windows like evil spirits that'd taken over. We were so far out in the country no one even knew there was a fire. I stood there, waiting in that cornfield until there was no house left. Somehow I thought my family might still come out. If I waited long enough my Daddy would rise from those ashes with my sister in his arms and Momma at his side. But they didn't and it was all my fault." I took a deep breath, not sure I could continue. "They found me the next day, standing in the same place Daddy'd left me, clutching the Bible in my arms."

Garland brought my hand to his lips and kissed the scar. He pulled me back on the couch and I curled up in his arms. I closed my eyes, drifted in and out of sleep. I'd never told Rudy this story and couldn't help wondering why this confession was so easy to tell to Garland.

In the early morning hours I started shivering. Not from the cold but out of fear. The story I had told last night came back to me in all its horrible reality. I'd lost my parents and sister because I played with fire. Now I'd lost Rudy due to my own foolishness. I had no life left to live.

Garland and I were still nestled on the couch and my trembling woke him up. "You're freezing," he said, rubbing my arms up and down.

"It's not the cold." I had so little awareness of my surroundings I couldn't even move.

"I know how to get you warm."

He stood, lifted me in his arms and carried me up the stairs. For a few seconds the cold of the storm surrounded us as he stepped outside onto the roof of the building. I closed my eyes, turning my face into Garland's chest until he opened the door of the greenhouse and a wave of heat hit us. Then, even as the wind howled, the scents of vanilla, jasmine and cinnamon blossomed like a candy kitchen. Garland laid me down on a stack of moving blankets and curled his body behind mine. The robe fell from my shoulders as the heat of the greenhouse moistened my skin. The warm air floated in my lungs. I looked up at the blossoms hanging over us. Dropping veiny sacs and ear-shaped leaves, pointed shafts protruding from ripe folds and dark orifices. Red, lime, deep shades of purple and scarlet, orange and yellow, some striped, others spotted. Aromas mixed, raspberry with freesia, and a hint of orange blossoms trailing behind as if hiding underneath. I inhaled as if a god were breathing life into me. Garland wrapped his arms around me. One thought kept going through my mind: If this life has ended, where do I go now?

Slowly I turned over, letting the robe open. I brought his hand to my breast. His soft touch sent ripples of tingling excitement through me. Garland gazed at my face and mouthed the word *beautiful* as his fingers webbed deeply in the layers of my hair. The floral aromas combined with the earthy smell of peat moss, bark and charcoal. Lifting my chin, I touched my lips to his. Not Rudy's lips, not his shoulders or his tongue. Everything about Garland was different, his mouth was wider, his limbs long and awkward against mine, but when he entered me I knew his power. He stayed with me right where I was, not demanding or serving his own needs. He molded himself to me and tears filled my eyes and streamed down my cheeks. Finally, I collapsed in his arms, and what remained was all I knew myself to be . . . Helen, just Helen.

18

The sweet, spicy aroma of orchids woke me up the next morning. Or was it the scent of cherries? For a moment I thought I had dozed off underneath mine and Rudy's fruit tree, then I realized where I was, in the greenhouse, in the arms of a man not my husband. A shiver went through me and turned into the nauseous fear of being found out. I sat up, holding my robe over my chest.

"Hannah?" Garland murmured, half asleep.

"What?" I asked.

He sat up as well and rubbed his eyes. "Good morning, Helen," he said softly.

"You called me something else."

He leaned against me and kissed my shoulder. "No. I said good morning."

I twisted around and looked at him, knowing what I'd heard. "Who's Hannah?"

His expression fixed like he'd walked into bright sunlight

and had to steady himself. He didn't seem embarrassed or fearful but more like part of him lived in another place, seeing another set of events unfolding before him. The muscles of his throat tightened as he swallowed, his focus gradually coming back to me. "No one." He pulled my robe around me and gently kissed my lips. "I'll make us some breakfast."

I followed him out of the greenhouse, across the snow-covered roof and into the chill of the apartment. I knew he'd deliberately avoided explaining but I also wasn't sure of being ready to know about Hannah. In the kitchen I'd be alone and have time to think. "You start a fire," I said, "I'll take care of breakfast." He thanked me with a nod and walked off.

As I broke eggs into a buttered pan, reviewing my actions of the last days did not seem like a good idea. My brain snarled with unanswerable questions. How could I have done this? What'll people say? What am I going to do? Stay here? Go home? Why had Garland called me by another woman's name?

One sickening fact pounded into my mind again and again, and no amount of rationalization could justify it. I'd betrayed my husband, my marriage.

Footsteps on the stairs leading up from the store squeaked gingerly like someone trying to sneak into the building. I looked around the corner to see the top of Cassandra's head as she peeked down the hall toward the bedrooms.

In a firm tone I said, "Breaking and entering carries five to ten in the state pen."

"Jesus, Mary and Joseph!" She squirmed like a cat being held over water, one hand to the center of her chest. "You're still here."

"Knowledge likes to be found," I said and shot her a squirrelly grin.

"Garland in there with you?" she asked, coming into the kitchen.

"Making a fire in front." I went back to flipping the eggs and held one up toward her.

"I eat mine scrambled." She leaned back into the hall to make sure Garland wasn't in sight, then closed the kitchen door and stood at the end of the counter like a praetorian guard. "Another storm's expected tonight. Ought to bring ten to twelve inches." She eyed me like a hawk on a squirrel. "You should be home before it hits," then looking down at the frying pan, added, "and put a little milk to that."

I stirred in some milk with the scrambled eggs, my back tightening.

"You stayed here to spite me." She looked away, jaw set firm, yet her tone wasn't bitchy and accusing. "And probably your husband, too. Maybe we deserve it, but Helen, you need to stop and consider the consequences of continuing this craziness. This is a pygmy of a small town. Think what people are saying."

"I've never been one to give gossip its due."

"I talked to Rudy."

I scraped the eggs onto a plate, laid a slice of toast beside them and popped another two pieces of bread into the toaster while making coffee, then realized I'd done everything backwards and the eggs would be cold before I could squeeze oranges for juice and heat up some grits. "Why would you discuss this with Rudy?" I blurted.

"Made the mistake of thinking he was an halfway intelligent human being who'd listen to common sense."

"I see no cause to insult my husband. In fact—"

"Save your breath, 'cause he told me off."

Now that sounded like my Rudy. I couldn't help smirking as I looked away. He didn't often lose his temper with women, other than me, but when he did it was usually because somebody was trying to force him into something he didn't want to do. I was fairly certain Cassandra's visit met that criterion. "I don't know what I'm going to do, but Garland has offered me a place to stay, and thinking is about all I'm doing."

"Make sure introspection is all that's going on under this roof, for your own sake."

I whipped around to give Cassandra a hard look but her expression didn't have the preacherish confidence I expected. She was sincerely worried and all my suspicions boiled over, imagining what she might be up to or might accuse us of doing.

"Garland's not for you," she insisted. "I don't want either of you to discover that after it's too late."

"I am not having this conversation with you."

"Oh, Lord, then there is a conversation to have." Her hands flew up into the air and slapped onto her thighs. She paced the kitchen and held a hand against her forehead.

"Stop," I said. "Just quit this." I set three plates on the table with more toast and coffee mugs. "I can only do one thing at a time and right now, it's eggs and coffee and I forgot the dern bacon!"

Cassandra reached out, grabbed my hands, shaking me and squeezing my fingers. "I want my brother to be happy, and if I thought it could be with you, I'd find a way to accept it. But you are not the person he loves."

"What are you talking about?"

"You need to take my word for this."

"You don't know what you're saying."

"If you don't believe me, look at the picture in his bedside drawer."

"I'm not going to snoop through his things."

"Well, I don't know why not; I did." Cassandra squeezed my hands harder. "Look at it. You'll see what I see. Then you'll know what's in his heart."

Garland's footsteps approached. "Is that Cassandra I hear?" He halted at the kitchen door, pushed it open and eyed his sister suspiciously.

She picked up her plate and wolfed down several bites of eggs. "Helen made some breakfast. Mmmm." She plopped the dish aside and rubbed her brother's arm. "Storm hitting again tonight. Reckon I better go salt my sidewalk."

"Cassandra?" He followed her into the hall, studying her like a law enforcement officer. "You're not pressuring Helen, are you?"

A warbling, nervous cackle was followed by, "I've always said you can't make a sturgeon breathe air. Haven't I always said that, Helen?" She didn't wait for a response and her clicking heels echoed down the steps.

Garland turned toward me, trying to assess my disposition.

"I'm know I'm not a fish," I said, and pointed at the table for him to sit. I chuckled in forced amusement like none of it bothered me, but I knew her presence had upset him. He must have realized my staying here was far from certain, if only because of community pressure.

We ate without speaking. He didn't seem to notice that I hadn't made bacon or that the eggs were cold. He reached over and stroked my arm. I was tentative at first but his touch had a calming effect. When we had skin contact I felt like I could breathe again. For a while, I didn't think about what was going on across the street and what had happened here somehow seemed okay, a world unto itself which didn't have to answer to the rules of society. I squeezed his hand and smiled at him. Part of me felt so shy under his gaze. It seemed odd to feel this way. This man wanted me. I'd made love to him last night, so I must want him too. It's not like I was the kind of woman who'd fall into another man's arms lightly, and yet, I had. Part of what bothered me was that it still felt so natural, so right.

When Garland went down into the store, I showered, standing a long time under scorching water. My thighs were sore but when I closed my eyes and remembered the sweetness of last night, I became lost in a swirl of heated images of our bodies pressed together. It filled my chest with a hunger I hadn't felt in years and left me eager and fearful at the same time.

For a while I stared across the street at the hardware store and I couldn't stop worrying about whether Rudy might suspect what I'd done. Then, the oddest thought struck me like a stick had smacked down on my head. He was across the street with Joan, and why hadn't she come over here to check up on Garland or me? What might have happened in our bedroom? I visualized Rudy and her alone. He'd kissed Rachel, but had he approached Joan? In his loneliness would he have been as weak as me? Would he have reached out to her?

"Stop," I said out loud. This was making me crazy.

As I passed Garland's bedroom I couldn't help but recall Cassandra's words, *Look at the picture in his bedside drawer.* I stared at the mahogany table with its antique silver handle. The drawer was ajar. I listened and could hear Garland moving around downstairs in the store. Against my better judgment, and straining against all the recriminations in my head, I stepped into his room and peeped into the drawer. The edge of a gold picture frame was visible.

Nervously, I inched the drawer open with a finger and stared into the eyes of a woman who could have been my sister. She was thinner than me, maybe five years younger, and had green eyes that stared above and beyond the camera. Her blond hair curled around her shoulders and her mouth was wide across her face and yet, she wasn't happy.

It was a strained smile like a sadness brimmed inside of her even as she tried her best to hide it. Hannah. This had to be Hannah.

That's what Cassandra was trying to tell me. I was a substitute for the woman he really loved. I even looked like her.

I sat on the edge of the bed, studying the picture, my brain numb. In the last two days my entire life had changed. I had made love to Garland and even if I wasn't sure what it meant, it gave me a place here. All the things that had happened to me since I was a little girl came back like steps on a ladder. I'd gotten through every difficulty. Somehow I always made things work out. What I actually wanted had never been something that mattered. If I'd gotten all my heart's desires in life then I would have had a mother, a father, my sister. Would have gone to beauty school and opened a shop. Had children and a husband who would have stormed over here and taken me back, no matter what. Nothing I wanted in life ever turned out. Not when I was a child, not yesterday, not today. But somehow I'd made it work, and I could make the best of this too, even if there was some ghost of a woman in the past. I had made love to Garland for a reason. It tied me to him and some part of me had intended that. I could make a life here. I had to. I had to because I didn't know what else to do.

19

All afternoon minor skirmishes flared up and down the street. Hinky Doolittle ran afoul of Leland Booth right in front of the store, and it took Reverend Studen to break them up. He lectured them right good about fighting, then turned toward the store window and shot me and Garland an offended glare. I could tell he wanted to say a few things but I guess he must have decided to wait and hope we'd all come to our senses.

Reverend Studen's lecture had as much effect as telling the grass not to grow, 'cause less than a half-hour later, Hinky and Leland were at it again with Yvonne Couasnon and Sara Lynn Elwood egging them on. Snowballs gone wild struck our front window and I jumped like a cat every time one hit. Marg Spilker's Roadmaster was set to get a busted windshield. Hinky yelled out something about the Bible being the law of what women should do, and Sara Lynn hollered back, "Kiss my atheist ass!" I wasn't sure they even knew what they were fighting about anymore.

Rudy and Joan watched out the window every time a new round of combat started. He would stroke his chin like he was deep in thought and I hoped he wasn't about to join in. Surely Joan would talk him out of it. As grateful as I was, part of me hated thinking a librarian could have such an effect on him.

Cassandra never came back to the store, but I saw her arguing with Rudy several times. Well, I'd warned her. Better he took his fury out on a nasty busybody than on Garland or me. As dusk closed in, the lights in the hardware store went out and worry threaded through my heart like delicate needlework. I couldn't stop staring across the street. My fists clenched and my nails dug into my palms as I tried to think of anything except the darkness in the hardware store.

"I think that last round was aimed at us," I called back to Garland, who was salting cornmeal on the butcher block behind the meat counter. I leaned as far into the window as I could and took in the disagreeable sight of bands of teenagers, grown men and even women bunched on opposite sides of the street.

Garland came up behind me. "How 'bout I take up some New York steaks for dinner?"

"Probably gonna be a run on steaks from all the punched eyes I've seen today." I couldn't tear my gaze away from the hardware store but pretended to watch Judy Koster and Bill Hitchcock skidding on the icy street, throwing hair rollers at each other as Hazel Robinson chased them and yelled they'd robbed her beauty shop.

Garland wrapped his arms around my waist, and I leaned back against him. My heart throbbed like bruised skin. Across the street seemed like an ocean away. I was here to stay. "I'll pick out some vegetables," I said and urged him toward the apartment stairs.

As I packed some mushrooms and red potatoes, a thin scratching vibrated the back door. Myrtle. I opened it wide to let him in, and he scrambled past my feet. Behind him, Rudy stood at the edge of the gate. My breath caught in my throat. His mouth popped open, just as surprised to see me. A sprig of fear shot through me. I wondered if he could read my face, know what I had done. Even if I had to lie the rest of my life, I would die of shame before admitting my guilt to him.

"I was trying to get Myrtle," he said.

"It's okay. Come on in."

He dawdled up the walk and stepped inside out of the cold. Myrtle settled down on the rug and stared at the freezer. "Come on," Rudy said.

Myrtle stayed put.

"Just a minute," I suggested. "Let's let him eat." I pulled the dog bucket from the freezer, and emptied scraps into the bowl and he commenced to chomping.

Rudy stared at Mrytle as if his hound was possessed. "How's that for betrayal?" He glanced over at me.

I felt as if lightning shot through my body and a hard swallow went down my throat. It took the strength of Hercules to keep my voice even. "He was old Mr. Cookson's friend. Kept him company."

"Funny day, huh?" Rudy pointed toward the front window where we could see Dwight Webber and John Johnson duking it out.

"It'll get too cold for them in an hour or so," I remarked, as if all I'd witnessed was normal.

He stared down at the floor, tapping his foot nervously. "Guess it's been a little too hot between us lately."

I swallowed and bit my lip. "We both have tempers."

"You know, Helen, what I said the other day . . . I didn't mean anything against Tansy."

"I know you didn't."

Quiet enclosed us for several seconds. My skin tingled and I almost reached out and touched him. He didn't look up at me as if embarrassed or unable to find the words he wanted to say.

"Well," he said toward the dog, "let's get home."

For an instant I thought I heard my own name, and stepped forward. But Myrtle trotted to the door, following Rudy's every move. Outside, he paused at the bottom step. I waited by the doorway in the icy air, half hoping he'd ask me to come home with him, too. Yet all the same, not sure I could make myself go.

"No, you don't know what I meant," Rudy said and turned to look up at me. He licked his lips, pressing them into his teeth as he strained against the freezing wind. "You know me better than anybody, and that's why you believe what I say."

"I don't read minds, Rudy."

"It was just the thought of a child suddenly being in that house. I always figured the first child there would be ours." I started to speak but he quickly jumped in. "I know how that came out, and I wish I could say it nicer."

"I wasn't sure you wanted children with me anymore."

"What?"

"I thought you were afraid."

He shook his head, confused.

"We're older now. I might never be able to give you kids at my age, especially a lot of them."

He stared at me, still unsure of what I was talking about.

"Remember that woman, Selma Hanks," I said, "used to trade with us before we got married, the one with the bunch of wiggly kids who looks like she's about to fall over from exhaustion?"

"Woman?" he asked himself as he focused on remembering. "Moved over to Harrogate where she could get daycare. Yeah, I'd say she could use a little rest."

"Last time she was in the store the littlest one chomped on your knee and knocked over a set of dishes." I bit my tongue, wishing he'd finish the sentence for me. "All those kids. Some women pop 'em out like biscuits from an oven. I didn't know if I could."

"Stop," Rudy said, holding out a hand. "I never thought that."

"But I— the way you looked at them."

"I never thought that," he repeated.

I stared at him. Sweat hardened on my skin as I came out on the porch into the freezing air. "Oh, Rudy. I thought you were thinking I might not be able to give you a pack of healthy kids. Maybe you'd made a mistake marrying me."

"That last day Selma came in... didn't you see the newspaper she had under her arm?"

"What's that got to do with anything?"

"She was carrying a *Knoxville Journal* with a headline about Andrew Riordan running for governor." His head drooped and he blew out a long line of frosty air. "I was afraid you'd see it. For a solid week after that I ran up and down the street grabbing everybody's papers, and I burned them until I read that old rich-boy Riordan couldn't raise campaign money."

It took several seconds for me to realize I was holding my breath. When I let it out, steamy white air mixed with the flaky snowfall and I couldn't help but let out a nervous laugh.

Rudy smacked one hand on a porch rail, knocking off a block of caked snow. "I was afraid you'd want to go work for his election."

"Well," I said, letting the word drop like wadded paper. "If he was at the capitol, and I was here, might have been worth it." Rudy bristled, probably more from the cold, I figured, but I still chided him. "How could you think something like that?"

"No more silly than you expecting I didn't want a child with you. Any child of ours would be perfect in my eyes, Helen."

"My campaigning days were far behind me by that time."

He shuffled his feet in the snow. "I guess . . . I wasn't sure . . . I didn't want to know what might happen."

"If only we'd talked." I couldn't help but shake my head at all the miscommunication.

Behind me, the door opened and Garland stepped out. "Mr. Ramsey," he said, "you're not welcome here."

Rudy jammed both hands on his hips and struck a lumberjack pose. "You want to throw me off your property, come on down and try."

"The sheriff made clear that you should keep your distance."

"Why don't we settle this like men? Better yet, like two dogs after the same bone. You game?"

I stepped between them and held a hand out in each direction. "Now, everybody, we can talk this out."

"Let's go inside, Helen," Garland said. "I've warmed up the bedroom."

"You what?" Rudy demanded. His cheeks colored scarlet. For a second he seemed ready to charge Garland.

"He means he made a fire upstairs," I explained.

"Is that all you meant?" Rudy jammed a forefinger at him.

"I have no intention of explaining myself to you." Garland stepped forward and I pushed him back.

"No, you don't have to, you've got a busybody sister explaining your psychology to the whole damn town."

"Rudy, that's enough," I said sharply.

Garland halted and with one hand steadied himself on the doorframe. "Your insults say more about you than me. But understand this, Mr. Ramsey, Helen is staying here and if Myrtle wants to stay, he can, too."

"Well, I reckon you've got beds enough for all of them!" Rudy carved a rampageous slide down the walk and kicked open the gate.

I held to the edge of the porch. "Rudy, don't leave like this."

"Like what I think matters? You're already sleeping in his warm bed."

"It's not like that."

"What?" Garland whispered toward me.

Rudy clamped both hands over his ears as if train engines were colliding inside his head. "If anything's happened, don't say. Don't ever tell me. I don't ever want to know!"

"Mr. Ramsey, go home."

"Might as well. Nothing here I got any interest in, 'cept my dog."

His words shot through me like a spear. "Then why bother even speaking to me," I hollered, my ire flying out of control.

"You want to know why I'm here, Helen," he shouted, wading half way back through a foot of snow. "I didn't follow Myrtle. I've known for years that he visits here. Every good dog's got to have his secrets. But me, no, I'm a damn stupid open book. I'm here 'cause I couldn't stand to let a day go by without seeing you!" He swatted a handful of snow off a rhododendron bush and stomped away. "You found yourself a warm bed, Helen Aubrey, I hope you burn in it!"

"Rudy, come back here!" I ran after him, angry, stunned and so touched by his words that I wanted to fall into his arms, admit everything and beg for forgiveness.

Garland caught up to me, holding me firm. "He doesn't even consider you his wife anymore."

"I have to go after him."

"You can't!"

"He's my husband!"

"You heard what he said to you."

"He didn't mean it."

Garland shook me hard, turning me toward him. "Hannah, don't go!"

Every one of my muscles seized up like a stalled car. He gripped my arms. I glared at him, knowing my expression must be showing a fury about to break, but it was his agonized expression that nearly broke my heart. "I'm not Hannah," I said.

"I couldn't stand losing you." Tears brimmed in his eyes. This time his face did show embarrassment, and he knew what he'd called me, but his mind couldn't distinguish between the woman he'd lost and the one standing in front of him. "Don't walk across that street. I need you. I'll die without you."

Until that moment, I'd never realized how damaged he was, how much Hannah had injured him. Life had wounded him far more than me. As much as I might have wanted to run after Rudy, I couldn't leave Garland Cookson standing there in the snow. Not in the cold. Not like that.

"Come here," I said, and opened my arms. I held him until we were both shivering. "Let's sleep in the garden again tonight, but please, just hold me. Okay?"

He nodded and tried to speak but the struggle for words was too agonizing. I pressed my fingers to his lips and pulled him inside. He'd taken care of me when I needed it most. Now it was my turn.

20

Early morning a commotion in the apartment below woke us. We scurried around draping ourselves with blankets and robes. A three-foot snow bank was packed against the greenhouse door but Garland edged it open enough for us to hop across the roof to the stairs. Once inside, the smell of bacon hit us like a wall. Voices were lively and passionate.

Garland motioned for me to wait but I shook my head and followed him down. At the bottom of the steps we were met by the owner of Troy's only gas station and garage, Irwin Vance, holding a plate of eggs and a mug of coffee. His eyes went up and down on both of us but mostly on me. "Damn," he said, "it is worth fighting for."

"Who let you in?" Garland demanded. Irwin nodded toward the kitchen.

Cassandra came out with a pan of biscuits and three other people followed her. "I brought help for our side," she said, walking past us. Just as quickly she noticed our state of undress, halted and turned around.

"We slept in the greenhouse," Garland said.

"For the heat," I piped up.

"Cassandra, what are you doing?" Garland turned in a full circle. His apartment was filled with people. With a baffled look he held out both hands toward his sister. She'd dressed in battle fatigues and wore a plastic army helmet that looked like it belonged to her son. "Quarter of the town's here."

"Other half down stairs," Cassandra said. "Couldn't fit everybody in up here."

She hadn't taken her eyes off me. I held the collar of the robe up to my chin but felt naked anyway. "Tell me you're not organizing these people," I said.

"This is not about you anymore, Helen of Troy. This is about . . . well, I don't know exactly, but I'm not about to lose the battle to the likes of Rudy Ramsey and his crew of half-wits."

"Tell these people to go home. This is not a war." I took a coffee mug out of beautician Maxine Norman's hand and pushed her toward the steps.

"You think not?" Cassandra marched halfway down the hall and pointed to the front windows. "Take a look."

Garland and I climbed onto the couch to peer out. Marg Spilker's Buick had a six-foot snowdrift on either side of it. Owen and Jimmy Lee worked at making snowballs and stacking them in piles. Several other men were building walls to hide behind and make their attack. Across the intersection, a diagonal snow bank separated Rudy's block from the Helen of Troy troops who were just as busy preparing for battle.

I jumped off the couch and glared at Cassandra. "The sheriff is going to arrest the whole bunch of you."

"All the way from Pruden?" She anchored both hands on her hips and rolled her eyes. "Sheriff Crow was wrong about one thing. We might not have our guns, we might be short of baseball bats, but I sure as hell will find another way to fight!"

From outside came the sound of men yelling challenges. We watched as Jimmy Lee and Titus Warner faced each other over the uneven snow wall.

"You-all's a bunch of cedar heads," Titus yelled and flexed arm muscles that won him the state high-school wrestling championship

"And you're a wad of butt-wipes led by a bucktooth soothsayer," Jimmy Lee hollered back.

"You hear what they said about me?" Cassandra leaned out the window. "Give it to 'em good, Titus!"

A volley of snowballs was accompanied by hoots and yells on both sides. As Titus turned, he took a blow on the back. He whipped out a slingshot and his snowball hit Jimmy Lee square in the forehead, knocking him out. Three boys ran forward to drag him by the shoulders into the hardware store. Titus and others on the Helen of Troy side raced out and cheered. I hunched over on the couch and covered my face. This town had gone crazy!

"There's only one thing to do," I said. Everybody leaned toward me as if their lives depended on my words. "I'm going to Maude's house right now."

"You can't leave us, Helen." Irwin stood up and stamped his foot.

Rhoda Knuckles knelt down at my feet. She was the first woman in the county to serve in the military and had a way of rallying the troops. "It'd be the worst thing that could happen. We've stood up for you. It's even husbands against wives. We've fought for you."

"This is not for me," I said, pointing at the foolishness outside.

"This is for your right to choose where you want to be." Rhoda stood up and walked in a commanding circle past all the people in the room. "Don't take it lightly. Rudy and every other man and woman has to respect your right. A person shouldn't have to stay where she don't want to. Everyone of us here believes that and that's why we're fighting."

"Helen, can I speak to you alone?" Garland towered above the others. He'd been silent the entire time. We hadn't even had a chance to talk about what had happened last night. I hadn't looked into his eyes more than twice. I wasn't sure how I felt about his feelings for Hannah.

We went into the bedroom and closed the door. I leaned my head on the burl-wood bedpost.

"Stay," he said.

"Lord, Garland, look at all that's happened."

"We're not about this. These last two nights were not about this."

I faced him. His eyes were dark as blackberries and lines of concern furrowed his forehead. "What was our making love about?" Stepping closer, I reached for his hand and we sat on the edge of the bed. "I don't think you know anymore than I do."

"Two people touching the depths of each other is not meant to be analyzed."

"Until I can say for sure, it's better if we don't complicate this situation anymore."

"You listen to me. Whether you're here or at Maude's, I will shadow you until your dying day. I will comfort you. I will cherish you. Until you tell me to go away, my shoulder is where your head will lay. I know I misspoke but I swear to you—"

I touched his lips, didn't let him finish words I was afraid to hear. I didn't think that in my lifetime I would ever meet a more tender man. Touching my forehead to his chin, I closed my eyes and went deep into my heart. A swirl of intoxicating fragrances came alive inside me, intense colors of blue and gold, and musical sounds that rivaled the sound of the sea. In a misty haze, a figure began to focus. I saw myself go up behind him and touch his back. He turned with a wide smile. I gazed into the bluest eyes.

Rudy's eyes. For whatever unexplainable reason, my passion was with the man who climbed trees to impress me, hung around back doors hoping to get my attention and got drunk when he thought he had lost me.

But now I looked up into Garland's face and his irises were a deeper blue than Rudy's. He hadn't shaven and the shadow of his beard gave him a rough look. I couldn't hurt this man. This soul who'd pledged to protect me deserved my loyalty and was not to be discarded as though what happened yesterday didn't matter. I wished I could talk to Maude. "I need to think," I said, playing for time until I knew what to do.

"Please don't think because I called you by another name that I don't know who I'm with." He cupped my cheek in his hand. "I wasn't myself last night. I know what we have and I know what I want and what we both need. It's not the circus out there. It's what we were by ourselves, the deep connection of us. I didn't imagine that, did I?"

I looked into his deep blue eyes and I searched my own heart for truth. "No," I said. "You didn't and neither did I. But I have to do the right thing, and I'm not sure how."

He kissed my forehead, stroking the back of my hair. "I'll leave you with your thoughts."

I dressed in my old clothes. Today I'd leave, go out to Maude's and end all this nonsense. One thing that bothered me as I looked out the window was not seeing Rudy or Joan. What kind of night had they had? I would rather have seen them out there making snowballs than to imagine them alone in our apartment. I went into Garland's bedroom and made a phone call.

"Rudy's Bunker," a voice answered.

"Let me speak to him."

"Helen?"

"Charlie Maxwell?"

"Helen, we're going to get you back. I was a witness when you were carried out of this place. I read all about the Stockholm Syndrome and brainwashing in a magazine and saw *The Manchurian Candidate* twice. Helen? Helen?"

"Put Rudy on the phone," I said with a sigh.

As I waited, I listened to the rumblings of battle plans as if something truly significant were at stake. Then, thumps of feet running up the stairs.

"Everything all right, Helen?"

"Why, Rudy," I said, "that's the first you've asked since this thing began."

"Well, there's been stories."

"I've only been gone two days."

"Seems like two years."

"Rudy, I need some clothes, some makeup and personal items. Tell Joan to pack for me. She'll know what to get."

"You're going somewhere?"

"Out to Maude's."

"That's a relief."

I waited. He was quiet. I cleared my throat and made a subtle suggestion. "What about Joan?"

"What about her?"

Sometimes my husband could be dense as a floorboard. "Maybe she can find another place to stay?"

"Why bother? She's a great cook and you're going to

Maude's."

"Rudy, you are as sensitive as a hibernating warthog."

"Am I talking Icelandic and you hearing Brazilian?"

"What's that mean?"

He was quiet for several seconds, either trying to figure out his own words or wanting to make me understand. "So, nothing has changed."

"If that's the way you feel." I disconnected the phone then started to dial again. A noise made me jump.

Garland watched from the doorway, his eyes as unreadable as Rudy's voice had been. One thing for sure, they were both driving me out of my mind.

Throughout the day several men and boys challenged each other and even the women and girls joined in the general mayhem. I wondered when they were going to run out of snow. Finally, there was yelling about a rock hidden in a snowball. Accusations of cheating flared up. I couldn't help but laugh. Somebody was upset about unfair play in a snowball fight. This town had found a new low. Cassandra's words came back to me, *I sure as hell will find another way to fight!* In a flash of insight, I knew what was needed to make everything right again. Cassandra had said it. That intolerant battle-ax might have made her first and only brilliant prediction: just the one I needed. *Another way to fight.*

21

I stood alone in the bedroom and imagined my strength. Everything came down to a simple decision: if they were going to make me Helen of Troy, then I would be that one-of-a-kind diva in all her magnificent splendor. I'd become the face that launched a thousand ships, the daughter of a god and most of all, I would bend the will of strong men and get exactly what I wanted. But first I had to find out exactly how the real Helen of Troy did it.

I dialed Maude's house. "Tansy?" I asked after a sleepy voice said hello.

"This is Tansy." Her voice sounded tiny and my heart went out to her. "Helen?"

"Honey, I have to ask you about one of your books. Remember the Helen of Troy story?"

"Rudy thought she looked like you, too."

I paused. Rudy had seen that book as well. I knew I shouldn't put Tansy in the middle of our fight but my curiosity got the better of me. "What did Rudy say?"

"I don't think he bothered reading the story. He liked staring at the picture."

"How did the story end?" I asked.

"She went home with her husband."

"No, I mean how did she make that happen?"

"They fought a war." I was quiet for several seconds. Tansy must have sensed my anxiety and continued, "You know what I think?"

"Tell me," I said, anxious for any kind of advice even from a ten-year-old.

"I think she must have batted her eyes."

"Batted her eyes," I repeated.

"Yeah, I bet she winked at boys a lot."

I thanked her and put down the phone. Standing in front of the mirror I winked my eyes several times. It came off silly as a goose trying to climb a tree. Angling sideways I did it again hoping for improvement. I still looked like a fool. I said a quick prayer, crossed every pair of fingers I had, then strutted into the living room and began barking orders.

"I need four guards and a bellhop. Miss Joan-Come-Lately is meeting me in the middle of the road with some personal items."

To my surprise five people immediately jumped up. I positioned them around me like points of a star, fluffed up my hair, and unbuttoned the top of my shirt.

Joan and Rudy waited on the other side of Marg Spilker's

Buick with a duffel bag and a plastic sack. No one had come with them and they looked uncertain as I marched out with my entourage. A dozen people stared from the windows of the store and apartment, including Cassandra's pinched and bothered face. I let my coat fall open so Rudy could get a good look at my shirt tied at the waist and boots drawn up over the bottom of my jeans.

"Isn't it a beautiful day," I called out. "The snow's let up and the sun's all bright." I looked up at the gray sky, then back at them—not a care in the world.

"Gonna snow again tonight," Rudy grumbled suspiciously. He held out my things.

I reached for the duffel bag, swung it over to Cecil Halsey, then opened the plastic bag and looked inside. "Let's see, shampoo, conditioner, facial cleanser. Oh, Joan, dear, would you mind running back upstairs and getting my pink bathing suit and my bottle of White Shoulders cologne?"

"What'da need a bikini for?" Rudy stepped closer, one hand on his hip.

"Why, sweetie, we take saunas in the greenhouse. You don't think a little thing like a snowstorm's going to stop us, do you?"

He stared up at the roof of the grocery. Joan's eyes followed his gaze.

"And perfume?" His mouth pressed into a thin line.

I glanced at Joan, then looked Rudy directly in the eye and winked.

"I'll be right back," Joan said.

"Look in the bottom drawer of the bureau in that bedroom where Rudy and I used to sleep." While we waited he paced, his arms crossed over his chest. I hummed "One For My Baby" then switched to "Santa Baby." Singing a few words then letting loose a long sigh, I yawned and asked, "What'dya have for dinner last night?"

"Fettuccine Alfredo," he answered proudly, as if he'd cooked it himself.

"Oooo," I cooed. "Well, I guess there's nothing you need from me." I winked again, then turned and pranced back toward the grocery. "Cecil'll bring the swimsuit, I'm getting a little chilly out here."

"Wait!" Rudy insisted. "I thought you were going to Maude's."

I raised a hand and waved it without looking back. Leave him wanting and wondering, I figured. Seeds of doubt, that's the best mystery.

"That woman!" he huffed in frustration. I could hear him kicking the snow bank.

When I opened the store door, Cassandra pounced like a stalking cat. "What do you have up your sleeve?"

I shrugged off my coat and Rosemary Duncan quickly picked it up from the floor mat behind me. "I have a mid-length, down-filled overcoat, Sandy, and there's plenty up it." I strode over to the fruit bin and picked up a shiny red apple. "Has this been washed?"

"I'll do it for you." Ricky Price took the apple and hurried back to the sink in the butcher shop.

Cassandra watched as everybody ran to and fro, attending to my every need, offering a chair, a shawl. "Don't make the mistake of thinking you're in charge."

I bit into the apple and savored its juices. "Who's our most dogged man?"

"Why, that'd be Conrad Scott."

"Conrad," I called out, and a shaggy-headed boy of about fourteen came running. "I need some new mascara. Could you run down to the drug store and pick me up some black velvet? Miss Rockwell knows the brand I use."

"I'll do it right away," he said breathlessly.

I leaned down and kissed his cheek. His face lit up like the sun. "Cassandra will give you the money."

Her mouth popped open. "I'll do no such thing!"

"Yes, you will." I winked at her then walked on and for good measure raised my hand and waved. It'd been an effective gesture with Rudy so I figured it'd irritate her twice as much. "I'll be resting, Conrad. Bring it on up when you get back." I stopped at the top of the stairs and glanced down, happy as a kid with candy that this winking thing had had an effect.

Conrad attached himself to Cassandra, holding out his palm. "Get away from me," she snapped and stomped off. The boy followed her, his hand still outstretched.

Well, I thought, Cassandra was right, he is the most dogged of our troops.

All afternoon people ran and fetched, doing their best to please me. Camille Sanders brought fruit salad; Daisy Jones

lent me her hair rollers and silk leopard print lounging pajamas; Ralph Williams built me a little footrest so I could sit in
front of the potbelly stove and put my feet up. After Conrad
returned with the mascara I sent him out again for lipstick,
at Cassandra's expense, of course. Even Mary Margaret
brought me a slice of carrot cake. I ate several bites in front
of her then flushed the rest. Finally, I ran out of things to
ask for.

Garland spent most of the day up in the greenhouse
tending his orchids. What had happened to his store and
apartment must have been frustrating to such a private man,
and I felt terribly guilty. All these uninvited people devoted
to their cause would not go away easily. If I had my way, this
would be over soon. My goal was to win back my husband
but I had to let it be his idea.

After dinner I took a long, relaxing bubble bath. I wasn't
sure what my next move would be. No new ideas popped
into my head. I fought off images of Rudy and Joan enjoying a gourmet meal. The old saying ran through my head,
the way to a man's heart was through his stomach, and she
sure had me beat on that one. While I dried off, thoughts of
them together crowded into my mind like unwanted vermin.
What did I have to fight with?

I peeked out the window, down into my kitchen. They
had just finished dinner. Rudy stood at the sink washing
dishes. I chuckled, thinking that at least if Joan had done the
cooking he was polite enough to clean up. A little swell of
pride shot through me. If he looked up, he'd be able to see

me. I glanced around, wondering how to get his attention. Tansy's suggestion of batting my eyes had worked but how to do it when I was across the street? Then, a sneaky idea popped into my head. A wily, sexy plan. An unfair play that if it worked would have my husband right where I wanted him.

I climbed up on the toilet and took the cover off the ceiling light. It made the room as bright as sunshine. I pulled the curtains tight so that from where Rudy stood I'd be a shadow. Slowly I shook my hair out, letting it jiggle all over my back. I let my towel linger over my shoulders and slip down between my thighs. Then I stepped back, flattened myself against the wall and peeked out from the far edge of the curtain. Rudy was leaning toward the window. Yeah, I thought, giggling to myself, he'll watch the dance of the seven bath towels.

I stood in front of the window and undulated my body like a snake. My hands caressed the full length of my legs from ankles to hips, rounding over my breasts and smoothing my sides. I pulled my hair up on top my head and revolved, letting all my curves show. Rudy was seeing all this in shadows and I wanted to send his imagination spinning. He must be wondering whom I tossed my long hair for. I let it fall a few locks at a time, drifting around my shoulders. For the finale I inched my face into the folds of curtain, holding the material tightly to my body. I gazed up at the moon, parted my lips, and gingerly let my tongue run around the outside. Then I flipped off the light and peered out again from the side of the window. Rudy's eyes were big as saucers. His mouth hung open. Yeah, I thought, I'm under his skin.

22

———

The next morning as I had breakfast in bed I worried that maybe I'd gone too far. What if instead of lust, I awakened disgust in Rudy? Maybe passion was something he no longer felt for me. Maybe he thought I was doing my hula for Garland.

Garland. I'd avoided thinking about him. While I dressed I decided he had to be included in my plan as well. But with him . . . well, more honesty was needed. He deserved that.

I found him in the greenhouse, the only place he could escape the hordes of acolytes and wannabe-warriors. Using a tiny paintbrush he dug into the sack of his spotted tiger orchid.

I took the brush from his hand and laid it aside.

He eyed me and said, "You could turn a epiphyte into a lithophyte by carelessly laying down a brush filled with pollen."

"I seem to have the power to turn mortal men into wild beasts."

"You're Helen of Troy, not Circe." He took my hand and led me among the hanging crystals. The light of the sun shone clearly through snow-crested greenhouse panes. Small rainbows danced around the room.

"For a while, I wasn't sure who I was." I reached up and touched a diamond-shaped crystal. "I found myself in your arms."

"I'll be good for you, Helen."

"No." I pressed my hands on his chest and looked up into his eyes. "I mean what I said. I found . . . myself." His face tilted to one side, eyes narrowed with doubt. I spoke carefully. "I know where I belong . . . and it's not here."

He turned away from me. "Did I do something wrong?"

"You could never do anything wrong." I touched his back and he turned around quickly, grabbing my arms and pulling me to him.

"I have kissed your lips, held you in my arms. I've been inside your body. I've seen your heart. Give us a chance."

I pressed my fingers to his lips. "What we are is not what's in your mind. There's something there, something I've sensed since I first met you. You're reliving a tragedy that needs a different ending."

He let go of me and stared into the sun. "That has nothing to do with you."

"Sometimes I think we mistake true love for what's only chemistry with a complete stranger who happens to be standing there, or some innocent nobody who gets in the way."

"This is not a fantasy for me," he said. "I am not putting

my feelings about someone else onto you."

"When we lose what we believe is true love, it's natural to look for a substitute."

"A lot of people in the world don't know what they're doing," he argued. "They simply know how to ask questions to make you doubt yourself."

"I know my heart."

He paced in a circle, his arms gyrating in frustration. "This is Cassandra's doing. My sister's confused you." Garland grabbed my hand and pulled me back among the flowers. "Let me tell you about these beauties." He touched a scarlet petal. "This one gives out a scent that mimics a female wasp. Once the male has landed, expecting to copulate with one of its own species, the flower hammers it until the poor wasp is covered with pollen and only then allows it to fly away." He touched a veiny, lime green sac. "This one emits a perfume so potent that male bees swarm around it. The unlucky ones fall into the bucket of the flower and the only way out is to squeeze through a narrow tunnel leading to the front wall of the receptacle. Just before the bee flies free, two masses attach themselves between its wings. He carries them until he dies or pollinates another flower. These orchids use insects, manipulate them."

"My situation didn't happen because the town manipulated me."

"Here in the greenhouse, I eliminate deception. With me you will always know what you have."

"Deceit isn't the problem between me and Rudy."

"You can't trust what you think you know."

"I will find a way to make you see the kind of man Rudy is, a boy in a lot of ways, and he could learn a thing or two from you."

Garland turned back to his prized flowers. If he was angry, he didn't let on. I returned to my room. What he'd said weighed on me. In a way he was right. I could not have predicted any of this. I couldn't have guessed that I would spend a night in this house, much less betray my husband. Or have imagined he'd now be living with a librarian. Everything was wrong. All the beliefs I'd held my entire life were in doubt.

Outside it had begun to snow again. When I went down to the living room, all around me people hovered asking if I needed anything. Janet Larsen was about to walk out the door.

"Where are you headed?" I asked her.

She turned hesitantly as if caught in a lie. "Thought I'd go home a couple hours."

"Not now. Not at the time of my greatest need."

"Well," she said, trying to avoid looking at the others. "I need to make sure my oil stove stays lit so my pipes don't freeze."

"What are frozen pipes next to serving Helen of Troy?"

"Of course," she replied humbly. Janet sat next to Mildred Prescott and folded her hands on her lap like a lady-in-waiting.

I cringed inwardly, sure that by morning they'd be fed up with me. Yet, the people in this store were only half the battle. It was time for Rudy to make a move, and if he would not, then one way or another I'd have to force him. I slipped into Garland's room with queenly grace, closed the door and called Rudy on the phone.

"Bunker," a voice answered.

"Charlie?"

"Helen? How are you?"

"Well, I'm so glad you asked. I've got a craving for grilled steak and was wondering if some of you might bring over an electric grill. There's one in the storeroom that's never been sold."

A few minutes later, three men staggered out into a blizzard, balancing a box on their shoulders. They carried it as far as the porch, where my guards opened the door.

"This is for Helen," Charlie said. "I want to make sure it gets to her and her alone."

"Hello, Charlie!" I called out from the warmth of the store. "Thank you so much."

"Anything else you need, you just call."

"You can count on it."

He and the others returned across the street. I glanced out the window, pretending to arrange my hair in the reflection. Rudy stood on the porch of the hardware store, arms crossed on his chest and his face flushed with irritation. Before the day was over the boys had brought over a steamer, waffle iron and three different kinds of toasters. Each time, Rudy followed the men, stopping in the center of the road like an Indian chief, arms folded, lower lip pouted. I was running his troops as well as mine. Neither side would deny me a thing. It must be driving him and Cassandra crazy. Good.

I knew a breaking point had to come soon. Early the next morning Garland knocked on my door and led me to the window. On their side of Marg Spilker's Buick Rudy's troops had a laid out a snow foundation of what looked to be a multi-room house.

"What's he doing?" Garland pointed at a team of boys building a snow pack into a high barrier.

I turned away from the window, my back against the wall and slid down to the floor. I knew at once what that arrangement of rooms mirrored. I'd described it to Rudy when we were in grade school, and I could hardly believe that he still remembered. "He's building an ice castle."

Garland paced in front of me. Confused and suspicious, he rubbed his chin. "Why?"

I felt tears rising in my eyes and couldn't look up at him. My hands covered my face. Painful memories laced through me.

He was by my side in an instant. One of his big hands dried my tears and cradled my cheeks. I moved closer to him and he wrapped his arms around me. "It's okay," he said. "Tell me."

"When Rudy and I were children . . . the year after the fire. Our teacher had us stand in front of class and tell where we wanted to live when we grew up. I gave a report on how I'd live in an ice castle like the Eskimos; that way it could never burn down, never again kill anybody I loved." I couldn't stop hiccups of breath. "I'd built it in my mind a hundred times. I knew where each room was, how I'd lay out the bedrooms and nursery, a library. I described every detail in ice."

Garland held me, rocking me gently. "You don't have to re-live those times."

"At recess the kids made fun of me, thought I was silly. Rudy was the tough little boy on the playground. When no one was looking, he came up and said, 'I'll build you an ice castle someday and you can live there forever.'"

Garland lifted my chin, holding my face still. "Don't you see? This man is determined to have you no matter what. That's what forever is."

"He wants to say he's sorry."

"Did you ever consider that he wants you back alive or dead?"

"This is small-town football not a war, Garland."

"Promise me you will not fall for this Trojan Horse."

Before Garland could stop me I ran outside. The cold hit me like a slap in the face. "Rudy," I screamed into a biting wind. "I see what you're doing!"

My husband emerged from a pack of men. He stared at me, his expression half defiant and half sad.

"We both see what you're doing," Garland said from behind me.

Rudy marched forward. "I've had about enough of you, Mister Fancy-Flower-man." Garland pulled me back and

Rudy exploded. "And get your hands off my wife when I'm looking right at you!"

"Listen to me—" I started.

Garland stepped in front of me. "I'm not the one who's had the problem with the roaming hands."

Rudy charged him, both of them slamming into a snow pack. I tried pulling Rudy back but my hands slipped on his parka and I fell backwards. When I regained my balance, I saw Rudy punching Garland in the face. He grabbed a shovel and swung it over his head.

"Rudy! No!"

He froze, holding the shovel high in the air. Garland, on the ground, raised an arm to deflect the blow. Rudy threw the shovel and turned toward me. "Is this what you want! Is this what you want? This! If you love him that much more than me then you stay with him. If you love him more, then you stay."

"Rudy, what have you done?"

Garland rolled on his side. He had a gash on his forehead and blood trickled from his nose.

All around us snow began to fall like rain. Rudy looked at his hands then up at me. "How could you have thought I wouldn't fight for you?"

"Don't you dare blame this on me." I went to Garland and helped him sit up. When I looked back Rudy was gone.

Garland moaned. Someone handed me a towel and I held it to his forehead.

"Thank you," he said.

"Garland, I'm so sorry."

"No need to be sorry. It was worth it, worth it if it saved you, Hannah."

"Garland?"

"Promise me you won't go back to him, Hannah."

The crowd gathered round us expelled a collective gasp. Someone cleared their throat. A couple of people coughed. But no one moved. "He's talking to you," Loretta said.

"No, not to me," I answered.

"Does it matter?" someone else finished a thought that must have weighed on many of them.

Garland touched my cheek. "He'll kill you, Hannah."

"Garland, it's me," I said and gently shook him by the shoulder.

"But Hannah, he threatened you with a gun. I'm afraid for you." Pausing and looking around, the jumble of faces must have confused him as much as his own thoughts. "I love you, Hannah."

A bewildered whisper rippled through the crowd, but my focus was on a man injured as much in spirit as in body. "I love you, too, Garland."

He looked directly at me, hands clinched to his chest as his focus returned. "I couldn't save her, Helen. It was too late."

I hesitated then said, "You must have loved her very much."

He halted as if my question was a fence in front of him. He swallowed, for a while unable to speak. "I pleaded with her, begged her not to go back."

"And Hannah didn't listen."

"So much pressure—her mother especially enjoyed being part of a wealthy family. She had no need of a middle-class, merchant son-in-law. So she shepherded this delicate flower into a den of lions. They killed her. That family murdered her long before her husband squeezed the life from her."

The crowd around us stayed silent; some bowed their heads as if to say a prayer for poor Hannah. If they understood how this past tragedy had played a part, none of them dared say so. "I'll help you inside." I anchored a shoulder under his arm. A hard pinch on my shoulder pulled me back as our supporters helped Garland up. Cassandra held me tight. I jerked out of her grasp. "I have to go with him. He's hurt."

Her eyes flared like a burst of flame shooting out of a rifle. "More than you know, you stupid woman! Don't you see how this little game has spun out of your control!"

I stood there, unable to move. Snow drifted around me and I felt like the loneliest person in the world. No way to reach out in either direction. I had turned Rudy into that horrifying beast, and now a man who'd done nothing but help me had been beaten senseless. The grocery store door slammed in its frame.

I looked over to the foundation of the ice house. Just what was Rudy doing? Was he building the foundation of a new life for himself? And did he mean to include me? I had trusted my heart, but too late.

23

———

They worked on the ice castle throughout the day and into the night. After the fight with Garland, I wasn't sure why Rudy even continued with the building. Was he trying to intrigue me, make atonement, or was it for spite? No doubt only he remembered my childhood dream. The snow rained down, leaving another three inches and providing plenty of raw material. Rudy's red shirt stood out even in the dark as he directed the others, constructing a staircase and a second story, but once a front facade was complete, it was difficult to tell what was going on inside. Oddly enough, from our side the entrance was through the back seat of Marg Spilker's Buick.

Garland had avoided me. Not so much because of his injuries, which thankfully were not serious, but more, I think, from his embarrassment about having revealed Hannah's story. I wasn't about to push him and while there might have been whispers, no one else mentioned it within his earshot.

Around midnight, Buddy Young staggered into the store and announced, "He's a crazy man."

Our people eyed him warily because Buddy had been with Rudy since all this began. He was drenched after hours of working in the snow, his hands scraped, his cheeks pink from cold.

Garland ordered a blanket to be brought and gave him a bowl of hot pork chowder. "What's going on over there?" he asked frankly.

"It's Rudy," he said through gulps of soup. "He's a tyrant. He won't stop. He's working us to death. We ain't even had any food since morning. He gave us a boiled egg. That's all, a boiled egg."

"Why isn't Miss Joan cooking?" I asked.

"He's got her making curtains for this house. Now I tell you, what good is curtains in an ice house that's gonna melt down as soon as the sun gets warm?"

"Is he planning a sneak attack?" Cassandra took Buddy by the collar and shook him.

"I don't think he's aware of the rest of the world. He's wild with this house. Said once he'd finished it, he'll let us go home."

"He's holding people against their will?" Cassandra asked.

"Threatened to close down our hardware accounts if we left before it was done."

"We're fighting a madman," she declared.

Garland looked at me, his dark eyes insistent and full

of meaning I didn't want to accept. I knew that he believed Rudy meant me ill. Quietly I went to my room, unsure what to think.

The next morning some of our people stood outside on the porch to watch the roof go up on the ice castle. Rudy's folks just ignored them. A couple of our boys took runs at the fence as if bent on destruction but veered off before hitting it. Their attempts at intimidation brought only joking from the builders and they invited the boys to help them. Ricky Price was so intrigued he switched sides.

Near dusk they strung Christmas lights all around the windows and door. It resembled a castle out of a fairytale, sparkling as if the walls were carved from crystal. Sections were transparent and holders had been drilled in the ice for candles, giving an inviting glow. I couldn't take my eyes off of it. It was the most beautiful thing I'd ever seen.

As I stood in wonder, Rudy and Joan came out the front door, his arm draped over her shoulder. "Hello, over there," he yelled at the grocery store. "You-all come on out. I have an announcement."

My heart was beating like I'd run a mile. My eyes were glued on him and Joan. His arm dropped down her back and he held up a hand to shush the crowd. "I'm calling a truce." He stepped down on the first stair of the ice porch and looked at each person facing him. "This is my peace offering. It's my way of apologizing for acting like a fool these past few days. I mean, we got this big snowstorm here and we all ought to be helping each other."

Joan looked on as he spoke, her shy demeanor irritating me more with each passing second. "Remember what I said," she prompted him.

He cleared his throat. "I think it's time we all got on with our lives."

"What about Helen?" Rosemary called out.

"What's between me and my wife will remain private."

A groan rose from the Helenites.

"But," he continued, "Helen is free to go or stay wherever she wants. I will not interfere."

Joan patted him on the back. I almost let out a scream.

Rudy gestured grandly at his creation. "So, anybody who wants a tour of my Ice House just crawl on through the backseat of Marg's car and enter a land that you won't see again until next Christmas." He smiled and several people clapped him on the shoulder. "Oh! There's one catch."

Another groan.

"There's a twenty-five-cent admission fee." Laughter shot up from both sides. "Well, can't blame a man for covering his costs."

People stared as if unable to decide to humor him or not. Conversation ran through the crowd like a surge of electricity. Finally Loretta Gerdau stepped forward to take the tour.

"You're not really going in that Trojan Horse, are you?" Camille called out.

Loretta hesitated at the car door, looked inside and

through it, then turned to reply. "If curiosity killed a cat, then it's got me by the scruff of the neck. I got to see the end of this. Anybody got change for a dollar?" she called out to Rudy. He told her to come on. She ducked, slipped through the car and came up in the front yard of the ice house, then looked at us and waved.

It took about twenty minutes for her to come out the back door. Joan and several others were there with hot coffee and muffins. Circling around, Loretta shouted to us. "It's beautiful. No traps. Nothing but ice, ice couches, ice chairs, ice TV. You're not gonna believe what they've done. It's worth seeing." She took a long drink of coffee as some of our people lined up. "Well," she added, "since it's a truce I'm going home now. See you-all." Her husband, Allen, who'd been on Rudy's team, came up beside her. They linked arms and hurried down the street.

"Wait," Cassandra called out. "It's a trick!"

I stepped forward, intending to be next. Garland caught my arm. "You can't go in there," he said. He pulled me back into the store and sat me in the chair beside the potbelly stove. "It can't be that easy. It never is."

"Did you see the way he had his arm around Joan?" The image pounded in my brain.

"If you don't want to stay here, then let me take you to Maude's," Garland pleaded like a child begging for candy.

"I have to know what's going on between them."

"These past days should tell you all you need to know."

"What am I going to do?"

"You need to listen to me."

"He's chosen Joan." All at once my insides flooded with a weary sensibility of hopelessness. I had lost. I had played my cards, bet all my money, and now, the winnings had been swept off the table in front of me. And I stood here with nothing . . . the loser in the game.

"I just can't seem to please you, Helen." Irritation filled Garland's voice and he slapped the stool rest.

"I know, Garland. I've noticed that as well."

A rap on the front window startled both of us. Rudy stood outside. He cracked open the door and leaned in. "Can I speak to both of you?"

Neither of us answered. I think we were so shocked at seeing him this close that our vocal cords froze. He stepped inside and sat in one of the chairs opposite us. Garland stood behind me.

Rudy stared at Garland's hands on my shoulders and I wanted to move so he'd not be touching me, but the image of my husband's arm around Joan kept me in place. "You remembered my ice castle," I said, an involuntary smile spreading on my face.

"Ice castle?"

"From when we were kids."

He looked down at the ground then back up at us. "No, I don't recall."

I pointed outside. "I used to tell you about wanting to live in an ice castle." I stared at him in disbelief. Was he lying or trying to hurt me? I felt all my hope melting under a hot glare of reality. This was the mess I had made.

"I got it out of Tansy's book," he said. "It's modeled off Mount Olympus, and I tell you what, it was an interesting place where all those gods lived, sitting up there like kids with puppets, interfering in the ways of man." He smirked as if Garland should be impressed. "Well, I don't want to bore the two of you with my hobbies."

"Why did you come?" Garland asked.

"I wanted you to know that I meant what I said out there." He looked away, into the fire. "I'm getting on with my life, and whatever you decide you want yours to be, Helen, it's okay with me."

I squeezed my hands together. "What do you want, Rudy?"

"I want you to be happy."

"And you're happy with Joan?"

He looked directly into my eyes but didn't answer.

Garland came around and sat in a chair to the side of both of us. "Mr. Ramsey, there are times when a man needs to speak his heart."

"This ain't my time," Rudy said.

"I suspected not."

Rudy looked over at him, not angry or even judgmental, as could be expected. Instead, he bit his lower lip as if Garland had reminded him of what he needed to do. Whatever pride held him was stronger than his manhood.

"Rudy," I said in a clear, firm voice. "I've decided what I'm going to do."

"I've been waitin' a long time to hear this."

"I'm leaving."

Garland looked at the floor. "I'll take you to Maude's."

"I'm not going to Maude's." I stood and looked them both up and down. "I'm leaving Troy. I'm leaving this mountain. I'm not sure where I'm going, but I'm never coming back."

Rudy rose and looked at me, such a yearning in his eyes to say something. Yet he didn't. He turned and walked out.

I followed him to the door and after it shut, I banged my fist on the edge. "That little librarian has destroyed my marriage."

"That's not being fair," Garland said.

"Whoever said I play fair?"

"Ah, but you do. It's one of your strengths."

"He's chosen her."

"But we'd have our lives. We can do whatever we want, go away, stay here."

"Do you think I could sit here and watch Rudy across the street making a life with another woman?"

"And they'd be seeing how happy we make each other."

"Stop talking!"

He pushed my hair back from my face then kissed my forehead. "Whatever you do, I'm going with you."

24

____

I packed my belongings, then went up and down the street talking to each person who'd been a part of my last few days, even those on Rudy's side. I thanked Ralph for building my foot-rest, returned Daisy's leopard print pajamas and all the other items people had loaned or given to me. Every loose end was tied in bowknots. I had only one more goodbye to say.

Maude and Tansy sat opposite each other in chairs beside the potbelly stove. Maude had nodded off and I knelt down on the floor in front of Tansy. "Maude's asleep," she whispered, and pointed. "I don't think she's feeling very good."

"Does she need a doctor?" Alarm spread through me.

"No, she said sleep gives her dreams of angels."

I gulped back a surge of sorrow. No sense getting Tansy upset. She'd had enough to deal with in the past days. "Honey," I said softly. "I'm going away, but when I'm settled I'll let you and Maude know where I am."

"Nooo," she whined. "Helen, don't go."

"I'm sorry, honey. It can't be helped."

"It can," she argued. "I don't want you to leave. Maude won't want you to leave and what will Rudy do without you?"

"Tansy!" I said firmly to hush her pleading and choke back my own tears. "Listen to me. Now more than ever, you have to be a very strong little girl. I need you to do something for me."

"Okay," she whimpered.

I held a breath and closed my eyes. "I want you to watch after Rudy." She blinked back tears but didn't speak. "You know how he gets hisself in trouble and nobody but you and me ever defends him. Well, with me not here, he might need you to speak up now and then." I exhaled, quivering with hurt. "Can you do that for me?"

"For you." She was quiet again then continued, "You know what Rudy always says, don't you?"

"Tell me."

"At times like this, when you're in deep doo-doo, you just have to make the best of things."

I chuckled. "That's what we're all trying to do, baby. I love you."

"Maude loves you, too," she said and looked over my shoulder.

I stood and looked into Maude's gray eyes. Her round face seemed to reflect feelings like cuts of a multi-faceted diamond. The years I'd watched it change from young to old flooded back in my mind: Holding my hand as she walked me to school. Posing me for pictures the night of my senior prom. Standing up for me at my wedding. I steeled myself and I could tell she did the same. Neither of us wanted to cry. Without a word we held to each other and I breathed in the vanilla smell of her, trying to memorize every second. Again, without a word she took Tansy's hand and they left. I watched them until they disappeared far down the street, not wanting to let go of the connection.

I stared at the hardware store across the street and whispered goodbye to a life now gone. The grocery store and apartment had begun to seem as comfortable as home. But it was also much more. It was the place I'd betrayed my husband and lost my marriage. He deserved my loyalty and I had failed him. Now he could have the life he wanted, and if that was with Joan, then I had to let him be. I had gotten exactly what I deserved.

I walked through the butcher shop and took a piece of cinnamon candy from the front counter. The rows of cabbages, radishes and cauliflower gave off a cool breeze from the refrigeration underneath. I moved to the heat of the pot-belly stove. This had been my thinking place and now my mind was numb. I put on my coat, pausing at the door with my hand on the knob. Once I walked out there was no going back.

"I'll pull the car around," Garland said from behind me. "I have us a hotel room in Knoxville. We can get a lawyer there to figure out what to do next, and then we'll decide where we want to go."

"What about your orchids?"

"I'll have to figure out what to do about them as well."

I pulled open the door and stepped outside. The crisp air gave my mind clarity but did not still the ache in my chest. My breath shot out in wispy curls. I walked to the edge of the sidewalk and looked at Rudy's ice house.

Oren Radley stood in front of Marg Spilker's Buick. One gloved hand swiped the chrome hood ornament of the Roadmaster. "They don't make 'em like this anymore," he said. He looked back at me, took a bite out of a square of chewing tobacco, and gestured at the house. "You ought to go through just once, sun'll melt it down tomorrow. Temperature's supposed to be in the sixties."

"You never can count on the weather when you need it." I stepped over to the car and he opened the door. "I'm short a quarter."

"Rudy's talking about doing this every year. It'd be an annual thing."

"Well, I guess he and Joan'll have themselves quite a little business here."

"Won't be the same without you, Helen," Oren said and looked a little sad.

I patted his shoulder.

A ways behind me Cassandra thundered out of the grocery store. She held boxes under both arms, carrying all her war supplies home. The sour look on her face was the same as the thousands of times she'd stormed into Troy Hardware, upset about any one of a dozen things. She stopped, turning her nose into the air, then glared down at me. "I know what's going to happen to my brother—" She caught herself and blinked several times. "You're such a great tragic figure, going down in the flames of your own lost cause." She marched on, a red banner reading HELENITES trailing behind her in the snow.

Oren and I looked at each other, not sure what she meant but figuring it must be profound. "She struggles nobly on and I just muddle through," I said.

He pushed the Buick door wider. "Sure you won't go through, just once?" Oren gestured invitingly. "Go on, no charge."

I stared at it, shimmering like a dream in the setting sun. The only ice castle I'd ever seen or was likely to see. Ducking my head, I entered the backseat of Marg Spilker's car.

On the other side I stepped in a patch of sand meant to keep the ice from getting slick. It was already watery from the warming weather. Each step further sent a titillating thrill through my stomach, like being a child given an ice-cream cone on a hot summer day.

The floor was snowy and had good traction. The remains of my flower planter stood on the front porch and had been rebuilt and painted. In the first room was a counter. Someone had carved a cash register out of a block of snow. It wasn't a living room. It was the entrance to our hardware store, built out of packed snow. I went toward the back and saw that the kitchen had been re-designed. A different kind of light shone from the block of ice used for the stove. I laughed at the sight of its electric burners. The rumpus room had been transformed into a child's bedroom. A small bed, miniature desk, teddy bears and dolls lay all around. What had Rudy done? I turned in a circle, looking at all the similarities and the differences. He'd changed our home into what I had always wanted it to be.

I returned to the front, determined to see our rooms upstairs. The first step crumbled under my foot. I kept going, slipped on the third step, fell to my knees, and when I caught myself on the banister, it cracked and dropped away. Oren was right. Soon the whole house would melt down but not before I saw Rudy's vision of what he wanted our lives to be. At the top of the stairs I heard someone entering the house.

"Helen, car's packed. We can leave." Garland stood in the door. He looked around, surprised by the interior, then came toward the stairs and held out his hand.

Looking down at him, I crossed my palms over my heart. "Garland, I need you to stand away from me, over there, on the other side of the room."

"What? Why?"

"Something's about to happen. I just don't know what."

He stared at me for several seconds then a gentle knowledge settled on him. One side of his mouth slipped into a curl of a smile; his eyes sparkled. "You're some kind of loyal woman, Helen of Troy."

"I hope you won't think badly about the things I've done or regret anything that happened between us. I will never forget."

"Nor shall I."

"I'm sorry."

His smile flattened and his eyes watered.

Mine filled with tears, too. I owed him more than I could ever pay and I didn't know how to say it any better than I had. Suddenly, a roaring shook the house.

"It's collapsing," Garland yelled. "Let's go!"

"No! I can't leave." The floor beneath me began to buckle. "Get out, Garland!"

He jumped for me but the ice moved, and Rudy vaulted from an open space in the wall and grabbed me, pulling me backward. We were in a dark tunnel falling downward.

"Yeee-hiiiii!" He whooped like a cowboy as we slid on a rollercoaster of ice.

We stopped with a thud, his back cushioning the fall. Both of us sat up in a tiny space illuminated by a flashlight stuck in the wall.

"Pretty neat, huh," he said.

"What are you doing?" I dusted snow off myself then smacked him on the shoulder.

"That man kidnapped you and I've kidnapped you back." Rudy wore an aviator's cap and smiled the silliest grin I'd ever seen. "Ain't'ya glad to be home?"

"But I'm leaving town."

"Leaving—" He halted mid-sentence and gaped at me. "But didn't you see the house? Didn't you see how I re-did everything? It's how you always wanted. It's the castle you used to dream about."

"It's an ice house, Rudy. It'll melt in the morning."

"But I thought if I could just let you see how I could be, how our life could be then you'd . . ." He looked down and swallowed.

"You'd what? Say it."

"You'd come back to me."

I re-positioned myself and backed away from him. "Seems like you've already prepared for other possibilities."

"No. I just wanted to talk to you, to you alone, just you and me without half the town involved."

"I think the whole town was involved."

He beat his hands on the sides of his head and pulled off the cap. "I guess that was my fault."

I snickered, covered my mouth but couldn't help laughing outright. "Wasn't your fault. You know how bored they all get during a snowstorm."

"Helen!" Garland's voice sounded hollow and far away. "I've found another way in. I'll get you out in a minute."

I turned to Rudy. "If you've got something to say to me, you better say it fast."

He motioned wildly with one hand as he struggled to find the words. His eyes nervously darted from the tunnel to me. He held up a palm as if he could stop Garland coming through. "I've done more than build this ice castle. I turned off the gas in our building and I've already started wiring it for electricity. Used my bootlegged cable wires. And I, I ordered a new stove to be delivered next week."

"Garland's is the only produce market in town. What are

we gonna do about groceries?"

"We'll send Tansy?"

"Okay."

"Okay?"

"Okay." I lifted one leg and kicked the side of the wall where Garland was crawling. The ceiling above it caved in, blocking the passageway. We fell into each other's arms, kissing as deeply as we ever had. Inside me burst a flood of passion I hadn't felt since we were teenagers. I pressed my lips to his ear and said, "Let's go home."

Every muscle in his body stiffened.

He held me away from him and looked at the collapsed tunnel. "That was the way home."

"Uh-oh."

We pounced on the pile of snow, digging until our hands grew stiff. The more ice we moved the more collapsed on top of us. Out of breath, we held on to each other. The flashlight grew dim and the air thinned.

We both put our backs against the far wall and waited. "Garland knows we're here," I said, rubbing Rudy's arm. "He'll get us out." I inhaled deeply, and my breath floated in a frosty mist. Again I sucked in air. So did Rudy. We looked at each other, both afraid to say what we knew was happening. We were totally enclosed and running out of air. I heard digging above but from the crunch of the shovels, I knew the sun had gone down and the ice had frozen solid. We weren't going to be rescued. They wouldn't get to us in time. Rudy put his arm around me and pulled me close. He kissed my forehead. What had I done?

"Rudy," I said.

"Yeah, baby."

"I have something to say to you."

"Anything."

"Make love to me."

If I didn't make it through this night, I knew in my heart I needed to die in Rudy's arms.

But we did wake up and I was astonished to find us naked in our own bed. For a minute I wondered if it had been all a dream, but Rudy came to a few minutes afterwards, kissing me hard and then telling me I was the prettiest thing he ever seen. That's when we saw it: a lit candle and beside it a large sheet of butcher paper headed in block print. I read aloud. "BE IT HEREBY KNOWN, YOU TWO HAD BETTER NEVER DO THIS AGAIN CAUSE WE'VE HAD IT!" It was signed by every person in town, all two hundred fifty men, women and children.

I looked up at Rudy and he had a silly grin on his face. I felt embarrassed, myself. "You know, honey," I said, "it's a good thing we're the only hardware store around, cause these people are mad enough to drive to LaFollette."

"We'll close down and open a daycare. I painted my rumpus room . . . pink."

"Well, I'm glad it's downstairs, no need it being too close to us."

"Shut up," he said.

I gave him a questioning stare. My heart, half-sinking, felt like it had been pierced, but his expression was reverent, as if in awe of how much he'd changed.

"The morning light's coming in over the hill," he said. "It's about to shine on your hair and make it shimmer like spun gold. I'll love you when it's as silver as the winter sky. Helen, don't you ever forget it. I'll never forget it again."

A warm feeling spread through me but Joan popped up in my mind like an evil imp. Then on the opposite shelf I saw the painting of me and Rudy—that wondrous double portrait, my hair flowing through the void to become Rudy's and to bind us together forever. It faced the bed where the occupants couldn't help but see it. I knew then that Joan had never slept within these walls.

And with that, we went back to sleep. We awoke, made love, then slept again. Sometimes we talked and wondered how we'd gotten out of the snow tunnel, but truthfully, we really didn't care. Right now, Rudy's arms were all I wanted to know.

25

——

Thirty years later—

Staring out the store window at the chrome bumper of a Ford pickup parked in front, daydreaming, something to do with me climbing a tiger orchid growing like a beanstalk up into the sky. Then I see her, Cassandra Dimsdale trotting her bony butt down the road like she owns the dern world. She stops across the street, looks directly at my hardware store, then here she comes. Great. She's seventy-two now, three years older than me. I've known her since third grade. She was a Harpy when she was twelve and she is a Harpy now.

"What's up, Helen of Troy?" Cassandra asks, flouncing into the entrance and holding the door open.

"You're letting out all the air-conditioned air, Sandy." I call her that 'cause I know she still hates it.

The glass door slowly shuts behind her and the little bell on the handle dings. On her pink shirt is pinned an oversized orange button with black letters that reads, Go Troy Tigers! Her grandson is the Troy Tigers' quarterback and most likely this year's valedictorian. Not really that surprising now that Troy's population is down to one hundred ninety-five and only twenty-eight are in high school. Most years there aren't enough boys for a sports team.

Cassandra slithers forward, her beady blue eyes doing their best to slice right into me. "You know I hate being called that."

I just smile.

She huffs out a breath like she's tolerating me and goes over to the crockpots. "These things have been on the shelf since Jesus was crucified." Instead of taking a basket, she picks up a stainless steel coffee carafe and anchors it under one arm. "Do you have any yard rakes?"

"There's a sale on straw brooms at the market across the street." Her back stiffens straight as an ironing board. Garland hasn't spoken a decent hallelujah to her in almost thirty years. She continues down one of my two aisles formed by racks of flower and plant seeds in the center of the single room. "See if there's one over there beside the snow shovels." I snicker to myself. As usual, she thinks she's come in here to bother me.

Cassandra returns with the rake and a self-satisfied look like I'd been hiding it all along. "You know they're closing the high school this year, sending all the kids to the county one."

"Well," I draw it out. "Probably good for them to get

some experience of the world."

"Pretty soon we'll be a hamlet of retirees and no-goods living on welfare."

I smile, but don't speak.

"Have to drive all the way over to Jellico to go to church as it is."

"Why, I just walk out into my backyard and talk to the Lord every Sunday morning."

She wrinkles what used to be a pert turned-up nose like she'd just smelled something bad.

I just smile again. I like doing that around Cassandra. It makes her pissy as hell even if she doesn't know why. All her life she's had her say before anybody else, and gotten her way by being a loud-mouthed, bossy know-it-all. I've always believed she was jealous because something happened to me that never would have happened to her.

I ring up the purchases and put the coffee carafe into a bag imprinted with the Troy Hardware logo. Handing it over, I smile a fourth time and gaze through the window toward the market across the street. Garland is outside arranging cabbages. "You ought to go over there and say hello," I remark as she struts out the door. The little bell dings and I think, round five thousand fifty-two goes to Helen of Troy.

Now, I've barely spoken to Garland in the last thirty years, either. We got used to not speaking and I guess decided it worked best that way. It was all my fault, really. Some old folks refer to it as the time I went crazy. Of course, I know better.

I figured all along it was Garland who dug us out of the snow tunnel that night. A few days afterwards I saw about fifty dead orchid plants lying behind his store. He'd probably yelled for every able-bodied man to help divert the warmth of the greenhouse and melt the ice. They all must have come running to help even though most of them were pretty mad at us. When there's a need, people help out like that in small towns.

For the longest time, I could only think that after all I'd put Garland through, what a good man he was to save our lives. It brought tears to my eyes. I suspect in a way Rudy knew too, but would never admit it. I sure did cause a lot of trouble back then. Of course, now I know I hadn't gone crazy. I was just changing. Oh, I don't mean physically or age-wise. I mean in my head. Rudy was used to me being like I was and I had to wait him out until he needed the person I was becoming. But I couldn't have explained all this back then. I didn't even know it myself. In the end it doesn't really matter if what seems to be the right man is a famous politician or just a genuinely good person. The man you'll be with is the one that gets your motor running. The man who'll fight for you, suffer for you and kidnap you from the perfect situation. It's the man who has a passion for you. Just last week, a few counties over, a woman shot her husband four times. He survived and when he came to in the hospital, surrounded by police, he refused to name the person who'd nailed him. You see, he loved his wife, had a passion for her and guess what, they're back together. I understood, though I guess not many other people did.

Rudy and I had a baby girl and twin boys before I turned forty-five and I reckon we were pretty happy. We built a few extra rooms and Tansy lived with us until she went to college. She's a doctor now over in Memphis. Maude was with us another two years. I think the whole county showed up when we laid her to rest. Garland ended up marrying Joan Jackson and they had three sons. Some of our kids went to school together and they all seemed to get along, so none of us ever brought up the past. We were content with things just the way they were. Oh, bad times came again like they do, I guess, with all people. Garland's wife died of ovarian cancer when she was fifty-eight. I was sad and sent two big pots of soup over to his house. He returned the favor two years ago when Rudy passed on, making sure a basket of fresh vegetables was delivered to me every week for a month. I've also noticed that on both their graves a fragrant tiger orchid blooms in the spring.

The death of someone you love is like a spike that tears you apart and for the longest time you don't think you'll ever come back to yourself. Love isn't freedom or letting go or independence like the talk-show psychologists tell you. Love is being possessed and its spark lights an obsession. Nothing can compare to it. I've come to realize that very few people ever experience real passionate love, and most of those don't know what they had until it's gone. Love that owns its beloved is irreplaceable. When it's taken from you sometimes you think it would have been better if you just died, too. Time is the only softener. It doesn't heal, it only cradles memories in a way that makes loss bearable. If you do end up loving somebody else, it's not a division of affections, it's in addition to. Rudy was my heart, but Garland was like a second skin as familiar as my own. Somewhere in between I discovered the treasures of my own specialness. I loved both of them and that passion was as big and deep and real as the blue sky above me. Love adds, it never subtracts. I believe that was as true when I was young as it is now. That's something Cassandra Dimsdale doesn't understand and never will. She makes a point of coming in the hardware store every few days to keep an eye on me and make sure I'm not chasing after her brother. But lately I've been thinking, isn't there an old saying about you can't have your cake and eat it too? Well, I've always been of the mind that if you can't eat your cake, what's the point in having it?

I walk over to lower the blinds so the afternoon sun won't fade the dishcloths stacked by the window. Across the street Garland is about to close down and go upstairs to tend his orchids. The day's been warm, not too sticky and I'm thinking I might just close down an hour early and go sit in my backyard, right in the place where I know Garland will have a good view of me.

THE END

About the Author

Author photo by Lisa Keating

Tess Collins is a coal miner's granddaughter with Cherokee ancestry on her mother's side and a legend of being descended from a mountain clan known as the Seven Big Sisters on her father's. Raised in the southeastern Kentucky town of Middlesboro, she spent her early years listening to mountain tales of haunted hollows, ghosts, moonshiners and unsolved murders. No doubt they influenced her writing. She is the author of THE LAW OF REVENGE, THE LAW OF THE DEAD, and THE LAW OF BETRAYAL, thrillers set in Appalachia. Her non-fiction book HOW THEATER MANAGERS MANAGE is published by by Rowman and Littlefield's Scarecrow Press. Miss Collins received a B.A. from the University of Kentucky and a Ph.D. from The Union Institute. She lives in San Francisco where she manages the prestigious Curran Theatre, a major Broadway show venue. Her web page can be accessed at www.tesscollins.com/